POSSESSIVE POLICEMAN

YES, DADDY: BOOK 16

LENA LITTLE

She's too young. She's my best friend's daughter. Staying away is the right thing to do.

But staying away is no longer an option.

Her safety is paramount. Especially now that her name is attached to a case of missing girls thanks to her Nancy Drew ways.

I'm here to protect her tonight, tomorrow, and always. Badge or not.

And I know what else she needs too.

She needs tough love, the kind of guidance, and sternness her father couldn't ever provide. Something I'm more than ready to give her.

I will protect her.

Because I protect what's mine, and that's *exactly* what she is. Mine. My little Luna.

MAILING LIST

Get free books from time to time by signing up for my mailing list...

www.subscribepage.com/lenalittle

LUKE

"But, Detective. You know the protocol regarding—"

"Mine," I grit into my dashboard mounted radio before slamming it back into its perch.

The other end goes silent, the Desk Sergeant wisely zipping his lips before I reach through this radio and put my fist through it.

I hit the lights, the red and blues flashing as my sirens wail. Laying into an abrupt, hard U-turn my tires squeal as I make the turn on two wheels.

With the pedal to the metal, I race through the straight strip of the city street like a bat out of hell, still too far away from her but closing the distance with each and every passing second.

My eyes dart left to right, making sure there's no oncoming traffic in either direction as I gun it through the rapidly upcoming light. Seconds later my tires screech and I'm parked diagonally across the handicap entrance to the police station that employs me in the town where I've lived my entire life.

Storming past the waiting area one woman pulls her knees up in a tuck and another man wraps his shins around the legs of the chair, both giving me a wide berth as my feet eat up polished tiles as I shoot past the oversized map of our city on the wall and the Rotary Club plaques and flags that are mounted next to it.

The glass partition that has to be spoken through to gain entrance to the station springs open, the click of it unlatching the only sound in a station normally inundated with the sound of phones ringing, doors buzzing, and file cabinets sliding open and closed.

I dart past the break room, other officers standing as still as statues, holding a coffee in one hand and some gripping the stereotypical donut in the other. The normal joking, chattering, TV, and microwave noises are non-existent. Delivery food sits half-eaten, chopsticks lodged in red and white Chinese takeout boxes. Even the office hardware seems to sense the severity of the situation, refusing to spit out rap sheets in the constant churn that it normally works in.

"What part of mine didn't you understand," I growl, grabbing the Fed by the throat and pinning him to the wall.

"Get your fucking hands off me, *local cop*," he hisses, trying to big time me in his navy blue windbreaker with the letters FBI in yellow on the backside.

"If that's what you prefer," I comply, releasing his windpipe and instead quickly putting my elbow smack dab into the middle of his chest, taking the air out of him. His body buckles forward, the smug look wiped off his face as he wheezes for air...and buys me a few more of the precious seconds I need in the process.

Placing my hands on the side of his arm, I sweep the arrogant prick aside. His absence from the one-way glass giving me a clear shot at my greatest fear...and my unhealthy obsession.

There she is.

My hand finds the back of my neck and I squeeze hard, the anguish eating me alive as I take in the sight of her delicate wrists encircled by the cold, unforgiving handcuffs that are used to confine hardened killers, not curious little girls like my best friend's daughter.

Her body twists, trying to find comfort in the hard plastic chair underneath her. It's a fool's errand, as those chairs were fabricated to make interview suspects uncomfortable by design. And I'm going to make whoever put her in that chair, in that room like a caged animal, a whole helluva lot more uncomfortable than they ever dreamed of.

Skin bunches around my eyes as my pained stare keeps me fixated on the little girl whose curiosity always got the best of her. But tonight, under a full moon, little Luna's curiosity may have taken her safety and security to a whole other level of peril. One I will not allow.

Serving and protecting is my life mission...always has been and always will be. It's who I am, my identity, my purpose in the world. And that's amplified a billion times over when it comes to her.

I grind my teeth and clench my jaw as I feel my toes curling in my shoes and a lump forming in my throat, cutting off my air, but not my ability to speak.

I stomp into the recording room where there's already a team of three people there ready to watch the interrogation that was just about to go down. "Out!" I command. "Everbody get the fuck out! Now!"

I look at the computers that record interviews and witness accounts, and my angel's face, up on the TV screen that show's the live feed is already up and running. But what needs to be running, and isn't, are the feet of the people I just ordered to leave. Wasting no time I grab them and forcefully shove them out of the room before jerking enough wires and plugs that the feed goes dead and the lights on the equipment go dark. At forty-one years old I'm the guy who's old enough to remember VCRs, but still can't remember how to buy an app on my phone…and never have.

When push comes to shove, literally as it just did, good old fashioned human ingenuity, combined with a bit of rage, can outsmart any damn machine any day of the year…especially when said machine is threatening to potentially harm the reputation, or future employment prospects, of what's mine. Not that she'd ever need to work a day in her life if she belonged to me…*when* she belongs to me. It's just a matter of time, I remind myself. She will be mine, but it has to be of her own choosing, a two-way street…not just me making it happen. I want her to be my everything, and she already is whether she knows it or not, but I have to know she chooses me of her own free will. And that she's not a bird in a golden cage.

My mind snaps back to the moment, and with a snarl and a few angry shakes of my head, I'm reminded that she's about as far from free will as a person can be about now.

Placing my hand on the knob to the entrance of the room I breathe out hard and slowly open the door, trying to contain

4

my nerves so she can draw strength from me. The last thing I need to do is elevate her already racing heartbeat, her nervousness, her fear. I need to swallow it all up like a whale opening its mouth as it swarms a school of fish. I need to take all that pain, that anxiety, that fear, and make it disappear in one gulp.

Here goes nothing. Correction...this is the most important moment of my life because so much of her future resides on it, and she's as far from nothing as one can be. She's everything. Everything.

It's time to do what I should have done a long time ago... what her dad should have done but never had the balls. No more waiting on somebody else to be what she needs in her life. This is the time to finally put an end to this recurring behavior that will only get her in even more trouble one of these days. The thought of something bad happening to her is devastating, and my lips purse, and every muscle in my body tightens in the second the fear invades my body. I kick it to the side, not even wanting to think about that, not even wanting to entertain the idea, the vision, of anything other than her in a light summer dress running through fields of amber wheat in the countryside on a summer's evening, while she catches lightning bugs in a glass jar...in complete safety, under my watchful eye. Always.

I know what she needs. She needs tough love, the kind of paternal guidance, and sternness her father couldn't ever provide. I will. It's time. I'm ready to be that paternal figure in her life, and a whole lot more. I'm ready to be her protector, her caregiver, her everything. Her Daddy.

LUNA

The absolute silence of the interrogation room speaks louder than words ever could. The smell of stale coffee, metal, sweat, and cigarette smoke lingers in the hazy air, illuminated by a single lightbulb, hanging just above eye level over the table.

But the second that door swings open a familiar smell, the smell of safety, cuts through the air and cloaks me like a protective shield, like my favorite blanket on a cold, stormy night filled with the crackle of lightning.

"You've been sticking your nose where it doesn't belong since you were a kid," the gruff notes of his gravelly deep timbre echo off the four walls. "You're not a kid anymore," he reminds me, a matter of fact, that my birthday last week means I'm eighteen now...and an adult.

He advances toward the table where I'm seated, the floor beneath him creaking violently as he approaches the other side of the Spartan metal interrogation device ubiquitous to the many movies I've watched over the years. Only now do I know out just how real, and how scary, it is to actually be sitting down at one.

Placing both fists down onto the table, and then twisting them in like screws, he leans forward, the light above me dimming as his towering presence, even when folded in half, kills the illumination from above.

Even so, I can easily make out the twin slivers of dark chocolate that narrow in on me from underneath hooded eyelids. His eyes may be dark by birth, but there's something light about them that glimmers as well. That authoritarian presence, and anger, visibly resigns as he just takes in the sight of me in my current predicament, and his control wavers, nearly vanishing.

Strangely there's a kind of excitement in his eyes too, even as they dart to the handcuffs that have me constrained to my current station in life. It's almost as if he feels this incredible sorrow for me, yet some sort of eagerness and anticipation about the position I'm in...and how he could compound it in ways I couldn't even guess, yet he seems to have already figured out judging from his quickly tenting pants.

A mixture of curiosity and fear tumbles in my belly as I wonder just how he'd use that throbbing bulge to make me obey. It's thicker than the nightstick the arresting officer put into my back, yet looks just as hard. Why would he have an erection now, and am I crazy or is he planning on using it on...me?

Does he get off on this kind of control, especially when it comes to...little girls?

My nipples pebble underneath the fabric of my dress, and I feel my skin turn from the sallow color that it had adapted to in this near dungeon, back to a softer, creamier tone. It's like this creature of darkness has given me light, which is as confusing as it is exciting.

"This isn't one of those damn Nancy Drew novels you're always reading. This is real life, with real consequences," he warns.

There's a rap of knuckles on the door, but his attention stays glued on me. The door handle turns, but it doesn't open.

"Unlock the damn door!" a muffled voice yells, but he pays it no mind. "The public defender's here and he demands the questioning be stopped."

Still no response from Luke, the star detective on the local police force, my dad's best friend, and the only man I've ever wanted, despite the twenty-three year age gap.

"Open up, or this could backfire real quick. The public defender knows you're her dad's best friend. This is all gonna get thrown out and we won't have a case."

The scowl on his face, the tight skin, it all loosens into a smirk. "Exactly what we want," he says quietly under his breath, but clearly loud enough for me to hear judging by his use of the word 'we.'

His body leans back slightly before lurching forward, the thick digits of one of his hands grabbing me by the back of my neck, his calloused fingertips showing little regard for whoever is outside that door and is worried I'm receiving some kind of special treatment on the other side of it.

The tips of his bared teeth graze my earlobe just before his nostrils flare and make contact with the side of my face as he places his Romanesque statue lips right at the entrance of my ear canal.

I can hear his barrel chest shuddering, like an approaching storm, but his lips stay closed.

My pulse pounds, my mouth feeling like it's stuffed with cotton.

The stubble from his chin scratches across my smooth cheekbone like sandpaper on buttermilk, sending my heart hammering in a dozen different directions.

His thick fingers move my head, positioning my chin into the crook of his neck the way one might hold a child.

A rumble vibrates his oversized frame and a gruff desperate sound slips from his lips.

"You know those animals out there want to make an example out of you...lock you up and throw away the key?"

"No," I whimper.

"Well, they do. But don't you worry. They'll never lay a finger on you. If they even try I'll bite the digit off and spit it in the gutter of the street, leaving it there for feral dogs to chew on." He pauses. "Some things are going to happen now that you might not be ready for, but this is the way things have to be. If they see me as weak, they might try and steal you from me, drag you back in here and ask you more questions than every quiz, test, and exam you've ever taken in all your years of schooling. And I won't allow that. I won't allow them to treat you that way, and God help anyone who tries to stop me." He pauses yet again. "I wouldn't harm a single hair on your perfect head." His reassuring words comfort me more than he could ever know.

"I—I trust you," I consent, my voice cracking.

"Come closer." His voice is firm. I have no idea how I could get any closer. His lips are grating my ear, his stubble scraping my flesh. I do what feels instinctive, natural. I move my head so my lips are closer to his, sensing he's not interested in talking anymore.

"Good girl. Now closer."

I do as I'm told until our lips are a hairsbreadth away. I can feel the heat of his skin on mine, my hands trembling as my knees knock together and the curves of the inside of my feet rub from side to side.

He mumbles a hoarse explicative, and I hear my handcuffs slide from my wrists, a loud thud as they find the floor behind me. But my hands don't move even though they've been set free. I should wring out my wrists, but all I can think about is bringing my freed hands up to his face and cupping his marblesque jawline, pulling him in for a kiss.

Just when I think he's about to kiss me first, his head pulls back, disappointment consuming me as a wounded sound tries to escape from my mouth, but I clamp my teeth down around it until my gums ache. The vacuum he's created, the void by adding space between us makes it feel like we were sharing a heartbeat to now being worlds apart.

As if recognizing my pain, and feeling it too, his lips come crashing toward me, like a scorching meteor headed toward earth as he stamps his lips over mine in a searing kiss that seizes my chest.

His need is so intense it feels like my body is on fire like he's seconds away from bending me over this cold, hard table and having his way with me right here and now.

Before another thought invades my mind, or I sense him losing control...his lips readying to invade my mouth, he jerks me straight up and out of my chair, hoisting me over the table as my chair slides away from where I was just sitting.

When a heavy exhale I come to rest over his wide right shoulder, which could comfortably fit three of me.

"Where are you taking me?" I question.

"On this table, if we stay here a second longer," he says with no irony in his voice, confirming my earlier suspicions.

"Watch it," he growls as he carries me through the door, his free hand cupping my head to make sure I don't accidentally bump into a wall as he makes a sharp turn. But I'm mistaken…not about his protective nature or his desire to shield me from harm, but as to whom his growl was aimed at.

The crowd of uniformed police officers parts like the Red Sea as he marches toward the door.

"Luna. I'm your attorney," a man says, trying to reach out for my hand to offer me his business card. My body spins sharply as Luke turns to face him. "Mine," he warns, his feet taking a wide stance. I can see his teeth bared in our reflection in the window of one of the offices as if he's a father bear protecting his cub. A sharp pain slices through my gut, his actions making it so clear that what he's doing now is the one thing my apathetic father never did. Luke's paternal instincts are clearly on display, as he risks his job and a whole lot more for me. My father wouldn't even risk missing one pitch of his favorite baseball team if I screamed that I was on fire in the next room.

"Luke. Everyone's staring at you," I whisper so hopefully only he can hear.

"Good," he answers, tipping his head back in my direction. "That means they're not looking at you."

Without another word he marches toward the front door, kicking it open with his boot. The doors swing open wide and he carries me through, straight into the parking lot and to his easily recognizable personal vehicle, a classic Ford Mustang that suits him to a T.

"She's a witness," someone cries out.

"She could have evidence, or tampered with it," another voice calls.

"You're risking your badge with this reckless behavior, *officer*," a third person condemns.

The world tilts yet again as my feet find the concrete below, my equilibrium twirling like a tossed baton.

With a series of grunts, he straps me into the passenger seat with all the ceremony of tossing away an apple core before the door slams shut next to me.

Not two seconds later he's in the driver's seat, the vehicle dipping and the shocks squeaking from his considerable weight.

Turning over the key, the oversized engine sparks to life, the power it holds clear even to someone who doesn't even have a driver's license, let alone knows anything about cars.

He yanks his door shut, causing me to jump, and a second later we're burning rubber out of there, surely breaking a multitude of moving violations in the process...and doing so in front of dozens of law enforcement eyes.

As we fly down the road like a bat out of hell I can't help

wonder if I'm trading one devil for another, but at least I feel safer with the devil I know...or do I?

My mind drifts back to that kiss, my heart still racing from the excitement of not only it but everything that proceeded and followed it.

Yeah, he's driving like a bat out of hell alright, although I can see he's a man firmly in charge of his machine. The only question is are we moving like a bat out of hell, or is this devil taking me into it?

And the even bigger questions...why does it seem so exciting, so new, so different, so heavenly?

So wrong, yet so right?

3

LUKE

Suspended indefinitely

I stare at the text message in disbelief, my eyes looking down and away, and then doing a double-take on the message.

"Are you kidding me?" I mutter under my breath before shaking my head.

Yeah, I just got suspended via a text message...apparently because it shows a confirmed read receipt, whatever the hell that means.

Who cares? I'd do it again in a heartbeat...for her.

I rub the back of my hand over my eyelids, clearly at a loss for words, and considering I specifically chose the pool table in the farthest corner of the pool hall I'm not exactly looking to listen to the words of others either.

But I get some.

"Sorry about that?" a voice says, and it's only then I register someone's jabbed me with the butt of their pool stick as they line up a shot from another table.

Mumbling something incoherent at the stranger's attempt to right their careless wrong, I move over to the wall and plop myself down on a stool, only then noticing someone's splashed the tops of my boots with beer.

How long have I been completely out of it?

Exactly seven days now...ever since Luna's eighteenth birthday party. Up until that moment, she'd always just been the bookworm kid of my best friend. She was more like a goddaughter to me, but something happened at that party... something I can't quite put my finger on, but it changed everything.

Her turning eighteen signaled her crossing the threshold of becoming an adult, and maybe that was the spark that made me look at her differently for the first time...very different.

She wasn't dressed in her normal attire that night. No. She had on this white dress that was so much more form fitting than anything I'd ever seen her wear, hugging the curves I didn't even know she had.

I wanted to put down my drink and walk right over to her, pinch a strand of her soft strawberry hair between my rough, calloused fingertips and bring it up to my nose for a long, groaning inhale, daring her father or anyone else to stop me.

But instead sat back in the distance that day, watching as she jumped up and down and patted her hands together in joy when she won the pin the tail on the donkey game with her friends, her hair spilling halfway down her back as she jumped around with that effortless childlike exuberance.

All I could think about was taking those vertical bounces and making them horizontal as I thrust into her over and over again, her hair lightly fanning out in every direction as I claimed that innocence of hers as mine.

I'm reminded of those baby blue eyes, buried underneath those curly long eyelashes, and how they caught me adjusting myself uncomfortably time and time again that day as I realized my buddy's little girl had become a woman seemingly overnight.

Taking a sip of whiskey from my highball glass, I let the amber liquid still in my mouth as the same song plays over and over again in the jukebox as a table of boys laugh, the only ones here enjoying their sophomoric display of annoyance.

These are the kinds of boys Luna should be dating, not an old hardened cop like me. Not a man who's seen death first hand, who knows the world is far from pure, perfect, and innocent...like her.

She's too young. She's my best friend's daughter. Staying away is the right thing to do.

But as I think of her, and how she's so wise beyond her age, I can't imagine her dating a boy like the ones before my eyes. And as my grip on my glass tightens I realize I'd find myself in prison real quick if I ever found she slept with another man.

The glass shatters in my hand, but luckily I only cut myself in one place and it's not deep.

A member of the staff is quick to show up with some cleanup tools and I discreetly slide him a twenty dollar bill for giving him work tonight that he didn't need.

How is it that a man who's been trained in controlling his

emotions...I'm a detective for chrissakes...how does such a man lose all semblance of control over a woman?

She's the only way who's ever made me feel this way and the feelings have only intensified since the first moment these feelings appeared last week.

The crazy thing is I can't wait much longer. I have to let her know how I feel. Screw that. I have to show her, and figure out a way to show to her father that this is real too. When I want something I go for it. And that's exactly what I'm going to do when it comes to her. I'm going to claim her in all ways, make her my wife, the mother of my children, my everything. Truth be told she already is, my mind constantly thinking about her and her safety. It's like she's crawled inside me and possessed every part of me, which is exactly why I have this need to possess every part of her.

I envision the softness of her lips, and it clogs my throat with lust and need. And when it comes to her throat why do I keep having this recurring dream where I circle my hand around her neck, applying just a hint of pressure to that smooth, slender column, until she begs for more? Until I press my thumb right on her erratic pulse and she comes all over my cock and I wake up in a cold sweat, heart rate soaring and my cock so thick and pissed off I have to walk bent over to my bathroom because I'm so needy I can't even stand up straight without being in pain before I unload my seed against the tiles of the shower wall? And in doing so I imagine those perky little tits and how I could fit each breast perfectly in my mouth, covering them in marks.

"Play ya for a pitcher of beer?"

I look up at the asshole who's just interrupted my fantasy. "I'm drinking whiskey. And I'm not interested," I growl, bringing the whiskey to my lips, reminded of how unobservant most men are. I see it every day as a detective, men who are completely clueless and unable to read body language, only seeing the writing on the wall after the crime has been committed. This is just another oblivious prick standing in front of me, and one who could have saved us both a lot of trouble if he'd just taken a second to think before opening his mouth.

"You win, I'll buy you a whiskey then," he offers, and my blood boils.

I want to leave, but now I'm pissed and I want nothing more than to kick his ass. Suspended from the force or not, I can't exactly knock him out and tip the janitor fella another twenty bucks to sweep him up off the floor.

"Rack 'em," I command, sliding off the stool and turning to the wooden rack behind me, grabbing a green chalk square and grating it across the tip of my pool stick.

The second he racks the balls and moves away the triangle used to line them up I thrust my hips with so much for the cue ball drills the first ball and then goes flying in the air as the balls ricochet in every direction.

It's then that he brings his drink to his lips, a clear liquid with a wedge of fruit in it. He's not even drinking beer? And for all, I know his drink might not even be alcoholic. Maybe he's a hustler, just wanting me to think he's drinking vodka. All I think is where in the hell did things go so wrong that 'men' put fruit in their drinks on every possible occasion?

I'm going to teach him a lesson about the differences between a boy and a man.

In a matter of minutes I'm mopping the floor with him, only

three balls left and I can take my victory and take off. I have no intention of taking free beer from him or anything else from anyone else tonight. All I want to do is let out some aggression and go where I need to be, where I should already be.

Closer to her. Protecting her.

I line up a shot that has me facing towards the front of the tinted window establishment. Just as I go to strike the ball, I catch a sign in the distance reading 'Minors Prohibited' and it reminds me that Luna was just that last week. My concentration is thrown and I hit the cue ball badly, missing the mark and opening up a chance for this young challenger.

As he lines up his first shot he leans across the table directly across from me, his shirt hanging open and the light from overhead catches the red ink of his tattoo and I can't help but look, seeing a tattoo of Orphan Annie tattooed on his chest.

What the fuck?

If these are the type of effeminate pussies women have to choose from these days I feel even more sorry for them than I did before…which was a helluva lot.

But as my eyes narrow in on the strange ink I notice something else that causes the wheels in my brain to turn over.

There's a scratch about four inches long running across the tattoo, and judging from the color and scab it looks fresh. Who in the hell would be scratching at a tattoo like that? The tattoo is clearly not new, and it surely wasn't done by a professional. Homemade…with no record of it, which just makes the whole thing in regards to this stranger…stranger.

He twists his body unusually, in a way not necessary to take his shot, but yet in a way that his shirt falls so it covers the tattoo and the invading claw mark.

He manages to sink a few balls but then misses. The turn alternates to me and I finish what I started, sinking the eight ball just as quickly as I jam my stick back into the wooden rack.

"Guess I owe you a pitcher of beer."

"Guess I best get going, son," reply.

"But you won."

I contemplate giving him a man to boy talk about how I'm always going to win in this world when pussies like him are my supposed 'competition', but instead, I let it go, knowing where my time is better spent.

Paying my bill and moving swiftly to the parking lot my attention swiftly returns to the only person in this world who matters.

Luna…and her safety.

My chest swells with pride as I think about how when she saw me today I watched her shoulders relax as if she knew that despite everything seemingly bad, everything was going to be okay because I was there.

Yeah, she was still nervous, but it was a different kind of nervous. It wasn't the kind of sadness and isolation that being alone in that interrogation room had given her. That's the kind that makes me want to rip at the flesh covering my heart.

If a single tear would have slid from those sad eyes I saw earlier today I'd be there on my knees, ready to sacrifice myself at her feet to make them go away. In the famous words of some dead philosopher, 'Know thyself.'

It may have taken me four decades and one additional year, but I finally figure it out. My mission in life is to make her happy, and in return, I find my ultimate happiness. It's a win-win situation if there ever was one.

Show me a single man on the face of this earth who's worth his salt who wouldn't be proud as shit over pleasing a girl like Luna. There isn't any because none exist. Not to mention only one man can be the luckiest one who gets that opportunity, that privilege. And that's me and I'll never forget how lucky I am to wake up each and every day to find new ways to surprise her, to put a smile on her face, and how that gives me energy, strength, and the desire to do something I *never* thought I'd do.

Start a family, but only because of her.

A few minutes later I cut the lights and the engine, and roll the last thirty yards down the street before coming to a stop along the curb in front of her house.

I'm not on duty tonight, and not even a cop at the moment for that matter.

But that doesn't mean I'm about to stop serving and protecting, especially when it comes to her.

My post tonight will be standing guard outside her home, the same place I dropped her off not two hours ago. The place where it took all the willpower I had inside me not to follow her in and tell her what she does to me, how she affects me like no other, and then doing a whole lot more than kissing her like a feral beast the way I did back at the station.

My beautiful princess is in that house alone tonight, a

reminder of the failings of her father as he prioritizes cash over his own flesh and blood.

I won't make that same mistake. Won't repeat his failings. Because together Luna and I are going to make our own flesh and blood, the most beautiful children the world has ever seen, entirely thanks to her and not me though.

She'll teach them how to be nice. I'll teach them how to be tough. And *together*, with both of our teachings and guidance, they'll grow into the kind of people that society needs more of.

Just the way I need her and want to isolate her from the world, especially while this killer is on the loose.

Do I think whoever this is is capable of harming another soul in our town, with the local police and now the feds on the case? Doubtful. But am I taking any chances that the prick could figure out a way to get to my Luna, especially now that her name's going to be attached to the case after what happened today? *Hell* no.

I won't allow it. Not. A. Fucking. Chance.

Her safety is everything and I'm here to protect her tonight, tomorrow, and always. Badge or not.

Because I protect what's mine, and that's *exactly* what she is. Mine.

4

LUNA

I pull the pencil from my mouth and tap it across the papers and pictures strewn across the kitchen table. "What's the motivation?"

"I just don't see it," Reggie, my classmate who also likes to solve puzzles and watch crime shows says.

"There's got to be some link between today's abduction and the doll found at the crime scene." I stare at the police scanner waiting for it to crackle with some new information, but it just sits there dead silent.

"You mean the evidence you were poking your nose in when the cops showed up and dragged you down to the station."

"I didn't touch it," I snap back. "And I had on the same gloves their teams wear, so just in case I actually did bump anything or disturb the crime scene I wouldn't have...well, disturbed the crime scene."

"You know your face is on the news now," Reggie says. "You could be a target."

I mumble something even I don't understand, sitting back in my chair and crossing my arms. "Thanks for reminding me."

"Just saying," Reggie adds. "I just don't want you to be endangered."

"I'm not. Trust me." I pinch a knowing smile as to the reason why. My protector, Luke. Anyone with an ounce of knowledge about this town, police work in general, or his protective ways would be crazy to cross him. I saw it first hand today and although I'm sorry I got him into that predicament, I can't deny that seeing it, being there firsthand, turned me on.

"You know he got suspended?" Reggie adds insult to injury.

"He didn't get suspended. They were just yelling at him to not take me."

"Suspended," Reggie repeats, pulling out his phone and holding up the screen inches from my face.

Now I really do feel bad. Real bad.

But I also feel a rumble in my bones and the shaking of the front windows, knowing that can only mean one thing.

"Is that him?" Reggie asks. "I'd recognize his engine anywhere."

He runs to the window but before he makes it there I cut the lights, which only provokes him more. Tucking his head around the side of the curtain he looks out.

"He's sitting just down from your house, but it's his car all right."

"Maybe someone else is driving it. You don't know."

Reggie looks back at me and rolls his eyes. "You really think

Detective Luke Noble is going to let someone else drive his prized possession, the car he's known for."

"He's known for protecting this town and solving cases. The car is just…something cool about him."

Reggie's eyes narrow and then a smile covers his face. He walks back toward me, wagging his finger in my direction. "You've got a crush on him, don't you."

"No!" I shoot back way too quickly.

"I never realized it until now. You've got a crush on your dad's best friend."

"Do not," I try and defend yet again, but my response is way too childish and transparent. Not to mention I don't have a crush. Luke is so much more than a crush. He's the reason I want to be a crime journalist and the only man I've ever wanted to want me. The only man I've ever wanted as my own.

"Whether you do or you don't you have an in with him. You think I can meet him?" Reggie questions almost begging like a puppy dog.

"I don't know. Maybe. I mean, why would he even come to the door or come by?" I fumble.

"To make sure you're safe. That's why," Luke's deep timbre reaches me from the other room. "Why isn't the back door dead-bolted?" he questions.

"We were just—"

"Who is *we*? Who is this?"

Reggie backpedals and suddenly his desire to meet Luke seems to have taken a turn south. "Actually, I'm nobody. I was just leaving." His chair scrapes across the floor as he quickly pulls it out so he can grab his backpack.

"Damn straight you were," Luke adds. "You have a ride home, son?"

"I'll call my mom to come pick me up. It'll only take her a couple of minutes."

From the scowl on Luke's face, we can both see that a couple of minutes is exactly two minutes too long. "Wait by the door until she gets here. I need to have a word with your crime fighting pal," he says, surveying the notes we have on the table.

"Yes, sir," Reggie says, recognizing and deferring to authority when he sees and experiences it in such a primal way.

"And, young man. Stop chasing bad guys and start protecting yourself and your family. Leave catching this kind of people to the professionals."

"I want to be a cop one day."

"It's gonna take more than one day and a lot more bulk on that frame to get where you need to be. I'm not saying you can't do it, and I encourage you to pursue your dreams but for now, just enjoy being a kid...and be safe."

"Yes, sir," Reggie says with a smile, excited that Luke himself advised him to follow his dreams.

Even Luke's head nod toward the door can't cool Reggie's enthusiasm, as he jams his things in his backpack and dashes toward the door.

"If I can get in that easily anyone else can too," Luke warns, his gaze turning to me, and turning deadly to boot.

"I know, it's just that...I mean I wasn't here alone."

"Might as well have been. You think some string bean boy's gonna protect you from the kind of madman that's on the loose. What were you planning on defending yourself with? A kitchen knife?"

I realize he must have already noticed the knife we had laying underneath our mess of information we'd been gathering.

"You don't bring a knife to a gunfight. And you're not in this fight at all anyway. You need to back off and let me handle this."

"You got suspended so you're not involved either." My rebuttal falls on deaf ears and I swallow hard, realizing why he got suspended. "I'm sorry."

"Don't be. I'd do it ten times outta nine. You know I'm not ever going to let anything happen to you, little one."

My entire body freezes at those words, that term of endearment. It's something my father never used with me, always calling me by my name, and only my name. Something about Luke is just more...paternal, always has been and it's like he's ramped it up to a new level since my birthday party.

The entire house sits silently until finally, Reggie pokes his head around the doorjamb and waves at both of us. "My ride's here." He pauses. "See you around," he waves at me.

Reggie waving his hand like that just looks...ridiculous with Luke in the room. The contrast between boy and man on full display.

"Keep your eyes on your own back and I'll keep mine on

Luna. She doesn't need looking after because I've got it under control," Luke adds, his voice serrated.

Reggie nods and makes a mad dash for the door. A few seconds later the sound of a car door slamming is audible even in the house, followed by the sound of it pulling away rapidly.

With one less body in the room the temperature should cool, right? Well, swapping Reggie for Luke definitely isn't anywhere near an even trade as the temperature in the room confirms.

The air grows thicker as does the expression on Luke's face. The slant of one of his eyebrows steepens as he looks me up from head to toe.

"I thought my dad was coming home tonight." I try and stand my ground a bit, but I'm not doing a very good job of it.

"I thought you'd wear more clothes when you have visitors over to the house, especially horny little high school boys after dark."

"It's my house. I can't be comfortable in my own house?"

"You think clothes like that make schoolboys comfortable or put other thoughts in their minds?"

It's only then I realize my yoga pants and oversized T might be a bit too...revealing, especially if I'm across the table from Reggie and leaning forward as we try and put the puzzle pieces together. He could probably see down my shirt. Correction, he could. And I can tell that's exactly what's on Luke's mind, burning a hole in his brain.

"Are you going to keep answering my questions with a question of your own?" I shoot back.

"Are you going to start taking your safety more seriously and stop showing off that tight little body to boys it doesn't belong to?"

"Exactly what I'm talking about."

"Watch your mouth, young lady," he warns, his meaty mitt grabbing me by the wrist and pulling me in close. My eyes jerk to his hand, realizing there's no way I could fight my way out of his grip if I tried for a hundred lifetimes. But I squirm anyway, waiting to see if I can so much as even shake myself free a little bit, but his bashed up knuckles don't give, easily keeping ahold of my wrist like a mouse in the talons of a falcon.

"You have random boys over when you're alone *and* when there's someone on the loose who's abducting girls who look somewhat like you."

"Just like me," I correct, annoyed that he's continuing with the questions but somewhat admiring that he's standing his ground and not giving in to my empty demands of a normal conversation.

"No one looks like you. No one."

"Reggie thinks I look like—"

"He's wrong, and I don't want to hear his name or any other boy's name coming from your mouth ever again. Ever. You understand?"

I nod, my throat feeling thick, tight...too constrained to speak. Luke's close proximity to me was doing a number on me. Sweat trickles down my back and quickly dots the valley between my breasts.

"When is my dad coming back?"

"Who would you rather have here to protect you...your father or me?"

His entire body stills as if the weight of the world hinges on my response. His grip on my wrist tightens to a point where it should be uncomfortable, but at this moment, in my twisted mind, the slight onset of pain shows me he actually cares about me, something no one else ever seems to have done.

Without even realizing it he starts to pull my body closer, or maybe it's my own feet selling out my true intentions, my needs, my wants, my desires.

Seconds later and his body is just inches from me, his dark gaze locked on mine. His body heat rolls off of him in waves, spearing right into me and taking my breath away in the process. I'm lightheaded, unable to think, to respond, yet that's exactly what Luke wants from me, demands I give him...the response he so desires.

His questions gave him all the power earlier, but now his latest question has flipped the table and put me in charge of where this conversation, this situation, goes next.

My eyes drift downward. "You," I push forward, my voice shaking.

His digits tighten on my wrist before quickly releasing me, apparently pleased with the answer he's received.

The void of his touch is quickly erased when the calloused tip of a single index finger finds the tip of my chin, lifting it until my gaze meets his.

"Up here, doll."

I say nothing.

"Why are you scared of me?" his chest rumbles.

"I'm not scared of you. I'm scared of the way I know you're ready to go about protecting me...the brutal way you'd do it without thinking twice or batting an eyelash."

"Only thing I'd bat would be of the aluminum baseball variety, and I'd be knocking skulls outta the park if I thought they even so much as had the thought, let alone the intention, of hurting you."

"Exactly what I'm talking about."

"Then why did you let that boy in your house tonight, especially dressed the way you are? I can see those peachy little tits without even trying, and that means that little shithead that was here before me probably could too." He pauses then grumbles below his breath but I can just barely make out his nearly incoherent ramble, "Should rip his fuckin' eyes out for seeing what doesn't belong to him, my innocent angel only for me."

The last part is nearly caveman level and as my eyes drift south again I realize there may be another aluminum baseball bat he forgot to consider...the one that the need in his pants could double as and I may have no experience, literally none, but I can sure tell that thing would do some serious damage to my body with a single 'swing'.

"I dressed this way because I know there's someone watching over me...always. I know that when other boy's eyes start to drift along my body they're reminded to look away...or else. They know who my guardian angel is and nobody wants to tangle with that devil. And knowing that they know it...it gives me a certain kind of freedom, power by association, and I won't lie...I love it."

"Guardian angel? The only angel here is the one I see in front of me."

I swallow hard.

"But this angel had been naughty, hasn't she?" he questions.

"No…Daddy." Shock ripples through me at the use of that word which I have no idea where it came from. Maybe it's finally my subconscious confirming, out loud, that I have the man I need that my father never could be…my caretaker, my provider of protection, my owner.

A guttural roll of thunder crackles from his chest the moment I utter the title, that pipe in his pants turning into pure steel, his corded muscles rippling underneath his snug white T-shirt.

"Don't lie to your Daddy," his language falls right in line. "Because that means you're being an even naughtier girl and you know what happens to naughty girls don't you?"

I shake my head from side to side, batting my eyelashes, and give him my best puppy dog eyes.

"Naughty girls get spanked."

My eyes go wide and my jaw hits the floor.

"Oh, don't you worry, little one. Daddy will be gentle. It's your first offenses and your first time." His hand raises and his rough fingers slide along my scalp before gliding through my long locks as he admires them all the way to the ends. "Well, my version of gentle anyway."

"What are you going to do, Daddy?" I ask, shocked at how comfortable this 'thing' we're doing feels…sounds…is. "Throw me over your shoulder like you did earlier and put me in bed for the night?"

"No. I'm not going to throw you over my shoulder. We already tried that earlier and it didn't work." He pauses. "Daddy's going to bend you over his knee and teach you exactly what happens when you don't do as he says."

In one fluid motion, he grabs me by the waist and jerks my body into his, sidestepping to the chair I was just sitting in and taking a seat, the wood creaking beneath him.

"No, Daddy! I'll be good."

"I'm not taking any chances. I'm going to make sure of it."

He taps the lycra spandex blend of my yoga pants twice, lightly, right over my cheeks as if to size up exactly where his big mitt is going to fall.

"Ready for your reminder?"

He cocks his hand back but doesn't bring it forward. Is he actually waiting on me to give my consent? Doing so doesn't dampen the fantasy that's playing out in real time. Instead, it gives me a feeling of more power, more control. It lets me know that no matter what the decision is always up to me, even though it's obvious that he could make the decision himself, and judging from his actions and ready state he already has. But it's that one last little piece, that final safety switch, that I have in my possession, which has to be pulled before anything goes further. And I appreciate it, and the thought he's put into it without actually drawing attention to it, more than he could possibly know.

I ponder a verbal answer but have no clue what to say. 'Yes' just doesn't sound appropriate. It's too bland, to not in line with what's happening, and beyond that has progressed at a clip I wasn't expecting.

Wiggling in his lap I clench my abs and elevate my butt,

trying to give it as much curve as possible so he won't be able to resist…and also so he won't be able to miss.

His erection grinds into my stomach and I feel a seismic shudder pass through his Herculean frame, his cock twitching in rapid fashion.

My airway opens and my thoughts fire, and I don't waste a second to spit out the words that need to be said. "Teach me, Daddy. Teach me to be a good girl."

A split second later all hell breaks loose and his open palm comes crashing down on my yoga pants, sending my body lurching forward, my neck stretching to its fullest length, and my mouth opening like a baby bird ready to accept food from its mother.

But there's no mother to be found in my life, and barely a father as my Daddy is proving to me at this very moment.

"You okay?" he asks, checking up on me, guiding me through this disciplinary process.

I nod.

"Just relax into it. You might find you enjoy it."

I want to turn around and slap his pompous ass right in the mouth, but I can't because I realize he's right. And his second spank confirms just that, landing in a separate spot, but this time he lets his hand linger, kneading my ass meat like a massage therapist searching for trigger points, and oh has he ever triggered something inside of me.

I feel like I'm awakened like this older man is teaching me something about myself that I could have never discovered alone, and certainly not with a boy my age. How quickly I'm understanding there's pleasure in the pain, especially when it's wrapped in my Daddy's worry, affection, and tough love that is only meant to make me safe, never to harm me.

"One more, so you don't forget," he grumbles, his hand coming down a third time and he kneads my globes like dough, delivering the pain and then soothing it away.

He massages my backside a little more before carefully adjusting me, moving me into a sitting position on his lap.

I have *no idea* why, but I take comfort by sliding my thumb into my mouth and sucking.

"You okay, precious?"

I nod and he pulls me in close, whispering into my ear. "Now, what Daddy needs from you is to stop wearing pigtails, French braids, and Disney T-shirts. And no going out after dark."

"You can't tell me how to dress," I sulk.

"I just did and you'll follow my rules or I'll put you under house arrest."

"Under what order?" I retort, knowing he has no legal basis for such a threat. I have learned a thing or two watching crime shows and actually reading up on criminal cases.

"Mine," he says flatly, with no regard for actual law.

"I'll have your badge," I threaten, my words rushed, crazy, and making no sense, especially considering it's already been taken.

"And I'll have your ass...again. Just remember you're never too old for me to bend you over my knee."

"Maybe I want that...sometimes," I blurt out.

"Then we'll have to come up with something you don't like, something to get you to mind. Sitting in a corner or writing sentences comes to mind, but if those don't work I'll go to the ends of the earth to find something that does because I'm not going to allow you to put yourself in harm's way. Not now. Not ever."

I say nothing, just suck my thumb some more which is still confusing the heck outta me.

"This is for your own good. You understand, little one?"

"Yes, Daddy."

"Good girl."

I wrap my arms around him and melt into his chest. The last thing I remember is the feeling of him carrying me upstairs and tucking me into bed, where I'm safe…because he's here with me watching over me, like always. Even when I don't see him or notice him, he's there.

Because he's my protector and now my disciplinarian when I get out of line. And most of all he's the one thing I never had but always needed…my Daddy.

5

LUKE

I curl a single finger around Luna's bedroom door, already worked up knowing she's inside. How I managed to stay downstairs on the couch all night is beyond me, but somehow I pulled it off.

I won't be able to do it again. Impossible.

And that's why I've been up since half-past three this morning planning out the perfect day for her, even though my thoughts were filled with all the indecent things I wanted to do to her in the middle of the night. Damn, I need her like the addicts I bust need their fix. Strangely, this obsession I have with her is actually helping me build a bit more empathy for the people who truly are addicts. Before I'd only seen them as a waste of space and taxpayer money, but now I know some truly don't have a choice, can't control their actions, just as I can't when it comes to her.

How I wanted to climb those same stairs last night, grab her thighs and spread them open, slide my tongue straight up and down her slit before sending it diving inside her. Just thinking about it now has me so hard I'm not even decent to answer the door, the pain in my pants evident on my face and on full display behind my zipper, which is struggling to keep my damn near already dripping inches of flesh contained.

I bring a single knuckle down on her door and I hear the squeak of box springs. All I can do is shake my head, wondering why her father hasn't put some of that stack of cash he has toward making sure his daughter gets a good night's sleep on a comfortable, modern mattress. Memory foam would be preferred since it's impossible to buy her a cloud to sleep on.

"Who is it?" she teases and I push open the door slightly.

"You know who it is, beautiful. Rise and shine."

"Looks like you've already got the rise part covered." Her eyebrows rise and fall as she tilts her head toward my groin.

"I'm a man. It's morning. It happens."

"I have a feeling not at that inhumanely large level for most other guys though."

"I'm not most other guys. I'm a man. Your man. And today I'm your tour guide to a day full of fun."

"What about school?"

"It's the end of the semester and I know the truancy officer. You're covered."

"A police officer is advising me to skip school?"

"I'm not advising. I'm ordering."

"You do that a lot."

"It's for your own protection."

"You had me at skipping school."

"Good," I growl. "Get dressed as fast as you can. We've got a full schedule ahead of us today."

"Yes, sir," she asks, playfully jumping out of her bed and saluting. The quick movement has her tits jiggling up and down against the neckline of her old oversized T-shirt, that's damn near transparent. Half of it is hanging over one shoulder, exposing her porcelain skin and delicate collarbone. How I want to trace its horizontal length with my tongue.

And from my angle, it's not even clear she has anything on underneath that shirt. What if I hadn't knocked and just opened the door? What if her body would have been flung out across the bed, her pussy on full display for me.

Would I have said anything? Would I have shut the door and ran to the bathroom to relieve the pain in my balls? Or would I have done so right there, spraying the carpet with my seed?

She bounces off to her attached bathroom and my eyes bounce around her room. How does she sleep in such a narrow bed? And how in the hell could I have mounted her in it without all four of its legs snapping in half?

Her dresser is lined with toys from fast food kid's meals. The adjacent wall is covered in books on a shelf that looks hand-made, or at least the decorations covering it are.

Most of the books are crime fiction but as my eyes narrow I see a few about specific police procedural cases. She must have printed these out in order to study them.

Another row seems dedicated to the ethics of journalism,

what not to report when a crime is unsolved so as to not hamper the police investigation, and a whole host of other topics.

My eyes continue scanning the room, seeing the stack of 'work' she's put together on this case sitting on a small table next to a hamster in a cage. I wasn't expecting that.

Next to her bed is a stuffed animal collection neatly on display, next to a stack of barrettes, hairbrushes, and sequined T-shirts.

The air smells like crayons and when I lick my lips I taste Watermelon Capri-Sun. What a helluva combination. Then again there's no one like my Luna, so why would I expect any different?

What's conspicuously missing are any pictures of boy bands or posters of men in general. Good. As it should be.

Maybe I overreacted when her little high school pal was over here playing detective yesterday. Regardless of his age or size, something about him being close to her was like a spark firing inside me, and immediately my anger was burning out of control. Just thinking his arm might have brushed against hers while they were spreading things out on that table, or maybe the little fucker was over here sniffing around thinking he was going to get a kiss...or more. All that jealousy comes roaring back and I know now I didn't overreact. I can't live with the idea of another man, or boy, even thinking he has a chance with my Luna.

And as soon as she finishes that shower I'm going to show her this is more than sex, more than wanting to have a family with her, for her to be the mother of my children, my wife, my everything. That in itself would probably be enough for most women, Luna is far from that.

She's everything. And I want her to achieve all her goals, which is why my first stop is to put her in line to do exactly that. To fast track this ambition she has. It's clear when she puts her mind to something she's not going to stop until she achieves it. I like her spunk. And that being the case I'm going to be right there by her side, cheering her on, picking her up when things don't work out, and reminding her that she's the best. Because it's the truth.

And if she wants to go chasing bad guys, and I know I can't keep her from doing it, what better way to allow her to do it than with me by her side...right where I belong. Right, where she belongs, tucked into my hip where I know she's gonna fit perfectly.

Now it's time to show her why I'm the perfect fit for her, in all ways. And that starts now.

6

LUNA

Tension and conflict slap me in the face the second we walk into the local TV newsroom, but what I feel more than anything is his Luke's hand settled right on top of my backside like he owns me.

It's as if he's showing me off to this unique world of important people I'd never have access to. Him vouching for me almost feels like he's announcing my arrival, letting them know I'm up-and-coming and on my way soon. He gives me that kind of confidence, without even bringing attention to it or saying a word, or asking for a word of thanks in return.

It's not something he does, it's who he is.

And what this place is is pure chaos. The sounds of cell and office phones ringing mixed with that of papers being shuffled only to be quickly drowned out by the white noise of many people talking in low voices.

The smell of coffee, although not as stale as that I experienced at the police station, mixes with the pastries that the journalists are taking a bite of one-handed at their desks while hunting and pecking out keys with the other.

Their computer monitors have sticky notes plastered on them and randomly interspersed amongst the desks are whiteboards with schedules and upcoming events. I even spot a few police scanners, one the same model as mine.

This is the fast-paced world I've dreamed of inhabiting, and seeing it up close and personal, thanks to Luke, is making that dream feel more like an achievable reality by the second.

It's the ultimate 'take your kid to work day' only I'm not his kid, and this isn't his job. But he has connections and judging by the way people are throwing around high fives, hand-shakes, and pats on the back, he has clout in this world too. I'm guessing they need him for his information just as much as he needs them to disperse what he wants to be dispersed, and keep quiet what he doesn't.

I can't even fathom the game of cat and mouse that must go on, as journalists try to dig for information that can make their careers, while Luke has to put on his poker face to keep things under wraps.

Off in the corner of the room, a man stands and immediately reaches for his back. His bloodshot eyes reveal he's probably been parked in that tiny chair, clearly not up to the task of supporting a man of his size, the entire night. After taking more than a few seconds for his back to fully straighten back out, and the wince on his face to subside, albeit slightly, he taps the heel of his hand to the side of his head, trying to relieve the crick in his neck from where he was just cradling a phone, the red mark from the heat it produced still visible.

Could I sit in a chair all night with a phone glued to my neck?

Yes, I could. Having Luke by my side makes me feel like I could do anything. And the trust he's shown in me, and the risk he's taken by putting his name on the line by bringing me here, only pushes my need to pay back the favor, the trust, the faith he's showing in me right now.

Without turning to look, he reaches back and takes my hand, his fingers intertwining with mine to let me know he's got me as he guides me through the rows of desks and bodies that are more like a zoo than a professional workspace.

We move to the broadcast room where anchors sit in chairs that roll and swivel behind a long desk. Textured walls help with acoustics as teleprompters tell them what to say while studio lighting makes them look their best.

"You can watch the live feed. There's a six second delay, but for all intents and purposes, it's live. Pull it up on your phone if you want and watch it play out after you already know what they've said. Kinda a weird thing the first few times you do it. I'll be right back. Gonna hit the bathroom."

His big hands swat twin curtains out of the way and his big body disappears into the darkness.

'COMMERCIAL BREAK IN 15 SECONDS' flashes across the teleprompter, and before I know what's happening, makeup artists dive for the news anchors while producers shout instructions in their ears...except for one rogue producer who shouts in mine.

"Look at the gift Detective Noble brought us." He pauses before shouting at the top of his lungs, "Get her into makeup. She goes live in the next segment. We're breaking this one on our network."

Stagehands run at me like their shoes are on fire and I'm

whisked away to a side room where I'm put in front of a mirror that would make Marilyn Monroe green with envy.

Two flamboyant men start cracking me up with their jokes as quickly as they paint my face as if they're trying to complete the Mona Lisa in under two minutes.

A man holding a clipboard comes barging into the room, shutting the door behind him. It opens quickly and another man follows.

"I don't know about this, guys," he warns, bringing his hand to his mouth and chewing on his fingernails. "Before he brought her in this morning he warned me to keep her out of the fray, and for everyone to keep their hands off her or he'd split whoever did straight down the middle."

"Pretty much the same message I got," the other man chimes in. "Although mine had something to do with my head being stuffed so far up my ass I wouldn't be able to breathe, and if he decided to show mercy later, and allow it, it would be through a tube attached to a respirator in intensive care."

That darn door flies open again and closes just as quickly. "What's the holdup?" the producer inquires, pressing a tiny earpiece into his ear as he seemingly listens to instructions and simultaneously carries on about three conversations at once.

"Not sure if this is a good idea," the man holding the clipboard says.

"Good idea? She was at the crime scene yesterday, is the daughter of the suspended officer's best friend, and witnessed the events leading to the suspension of the one and only man the public feels is capable of bringing this whacko to justice. And we've got an exclusive. What's not good about that?" He taps his foot and jets his head out toward the man, addressing him as if his thought is the most asinine he's ever heard.

And then we all hear the reason why it's not.

"Luna!" a voice so cold it's scarier than any murderer could ever hope to be, calls out...Luke realizing I'm not where he left me.

Fear spreads in my chest, but not for me...for the pushy producer.

"Don't say a word. We can get her on without him knowing. Use the side exit.

"Luna!" he calls out again.

"That's not a good idea," I inform, hoping this greedy producer gets the message before it's delivered with fists instead of words.

Suddenly the doorknob shakes violently in all directions.

"Awww shit. Run!" one of the men says, but it's too late.

The door comes crashing in, Luke's boot smashing through the thin particle board, which never had a chance. He throws his shoulder into it for good measure and all three hinges collapse, the door falling forward into the room and Luke stepping right on top of it as if he was Clint Eastwood about to enter a saloon and shoot all the bad guys dead in six pulls of the trigger...or less.

Luke's eyes sweep the room as he sizes up the situation like a S.W.A.T. point man entering a drug dealer's stash house. His hands jet out sideways, pushing into the frame as he groans at the top of his lungs, causing us all to bring our hands to our ears to block out the sound.

"She's not part of this," he growls at the producer. I run right at him, wrapping myself around his right arm, his dominant one, so instead, he grabs the producer by the neck with his left and lifts him clean up off the floor.

"You kicked the door down," I say in awe.

"It was standing between me and you," he says as if it's the most obvious course of action in such a situation, his eyes never leaving the unnamed producer.

"No one is putting my girl on the air, serving her up for ratings or worse yet for that deranged prick out there who's still on the loose."

"O—okay," the producer manages to choke out, his face turning from red to purple.

"Didn't I make that clear before we came in this morning?"

"Uh-huh," he says, and Luke releases him, his body falling to the ground like a spineless jellyfish, a mess of appendages on the floor.

"I should have known something like this would happen," he snaps. "Should have known these other pricks would covet what's mine and try and use my goodwill against me. That's the thing about being the top dog on the sled team. Everyone else's view is always the same so they're always gunning for you, always trying to knock you back to get some of that fresh air instead of just brown-nosing you all damn day. Little fuckers always trying to take advantage when they should just shut the hell up and thank me, or pick up a weapon and get out there on the street themselves, roll around in the mud with the pigs like I do, and hunt down these sick bastards on their own like I've been doing for coming on twenty years now. But they can't, so they won't."

Luke scoops me up and tucks me into his hip. I'm not sure if I feel ashamed that I can't take care of myself in these situations or protected beyond belief. Maybe a little of both, which is confusing. I think it stems from the fact that I hoped to be a part of this fraternity one day, and I don't need to be looked at as someone who can't fight her own battles...even though the whole world knows I'll never need to on my own as long as Luke has air in his lungs.

Stepping over the producer he moves back toward the now wide open entryway, but pauses before turning back to address the remaining crowd of shocked onlookers, glad they weren't made an example of like the man who's still rubbing his throat in the fetal position two steps behind us.

"Any of you so much as go near her again without my permission and I'll saw your dick off with a rusty butter knife. Or better yet I'll tie you up to a chair in a dark dingy basement, and you know this good detective knows of more than a few, and let a homeless crackhead with a single tooth do the honors while I blast heavy metal into your skull through noise canceling headphones...until he's gnawed the toothpicks you effeminate low testosterone pansies squat to piss out of clean off. Are we clear?"

They all nod furiously.

"Are. We. Clear?"

"Yes, Detective!" they sound off in unison as if they were suddenly transformed into a well-rehearsed Marine Corps recruit battalion and he was their Senior Drill Instructor.

"She's *mine*. Not yours. Not anybody else's but mine," he snarls, carrying me out of the makeup room, through the broadcasting room, and out the front door, as I watch men's head fall forward like the rope that was holding them up was cut, as their eyes dart for the floor in submission as Luke passes them by.

The scurrying newspeople are now diving for cover. There's a story for ya. Who would have known?

And I'm filled with warmth from the knowledge that I've been possessed. I'm his girl. He claimed me loud in clear in front of the single largest group of people that control what the city hears, and in this case, the country as all eyes are turning to this manhunt. But I'll never need to hunt for a man myself because I've clearly got the biggest, brashest in my corner.

My possessive policeman. And I belong to him and only him.

7

LUKE

No good deed goes unpunished?

I tried to do a good deed and was punished by those selfish pricks who wanted to take advantage of my princess. But I'm no worse for the wear, or at least I'm going to keep repeating it until I believe it.

The real punishment is the one I dished out back at the newsroom. But it's time to put that behind me and move on to the second part of our date. Time to take a step back and cool down.

After giving her a glimpse of the future she wants so desperately, it's time to flip the script and give her a look at the childhood she never had.

"Which one do you want to ride first?" I ask, extending both arms to let her know the amusement park is her playground for the next hour, two hours, three hours, four...however long she wants it to be.

Seconds later we're on a teacup ride and I can only imagine

how silly someone my size must look with my knees tucked up to my throat. As we spin around, and I contemplate why this ride, of all rides, was the first one we went on, I see myself in a mirror. And I see something I haven't seen in a very, very long time.

A smile plastered across my face.

Something about her childlike exuberance just wears off on me, affects me, and as I look across the other side of the teacup and see her head tilted back and her hair flowing in every which direction I know she's experiencing pure bliss.

Bliss? Since when did that kind of word ever so much as enter my head as a thought? Since her, that's when.

Over the next hour, we ride bumper boats firing water gun cannons at other boaters in a man-made pool, where I'm careful to block all incoming water. No way I'm letting her shirt get wet and part of her body to be revealed to anyone other than me.

We move on to a dumbbell strength meter, which I break when I smash it...guess it wasn't ready for me. After that, there's a kiddie ball pit and climbing area, rows of carnival games like a ring toss with giant stuffed animals hanging from the ceiling as prizes, and I'm obsessed with winning her the biggest one.

Three tries later and we're walking away with a teddy bear that's as big as she is, making room for him as we sit down on a bench and stuff our faces with pizza and cotton candy, while drinking slushes. I toss my straw in the trash though, some habits will never die.

"Are you having fun?" she asks me as if the answer isn't the most obvious in the world.

"With you, I could be trapped inside a soggy cardboard box and have the time of life, every time," I say, just shaking my head as I can't believe my luck as I take in her beauty over the loud music, laughter, bells dinging and children screaming. It all just blurs into the background. The only thing I see, hear, feel, can think about…is her.

"Can I ask you one other question?"

"Always?"

"Why are you so protective?"

It's a good question, and a fair one. I look down at my hands, not sure where to begin. Buying a few seconds by scraping away some paint that slid underneath one of my fingernails from one of the safety bar rides, I think back to how I was holding it tight, just in case. Even though it was locked in, no way was I going to let it malfunction and something happen to my woman.

I grab a napkin and carefully dab at the pink cotton candy that's found it's way to her too cute nose and then exhale and begin.

"Something happened when I was younger, and as I later learned from my training, of all the wounds we experience in life, childhood-specific ones can do the most damage, since the younger the victim is, the fewer emotional barriers are in place for protection." I take another deep breath and slowly let it out. "I'm so protective because sometimes that's what other people need, especially those close to me. Specifically, I wasn't able to protect my mother from my father, no matter how hard I tried."

Her tiny hand finds the top of mine. "We don't have to talk about it if you don't want to."

"It's okay. You should know what makes me, me. My father was abusive to both my mother and me, mostly her, but my mother wouldn't report him because that's what she thought love was…abuse. She saw her father do it to her mother so it repeated itself in her own relationship later in life. Back then I looked a lot more like David than Goliath, as I do today. And I definitely felt small when I was hanging onto my dad's pant leg, biting into it, my teeth breaking through the fabric and his flesh, trying anything so he'd take his hands off my mother, only for him to swat me away like a fly, but to make matters worse he liked to use a frying pan to do so…sometimes fresh from the stove."

"That sounds terrible."

"It was worse for my mother, believe it or not. One day I'd had enough. I was going to protect my mom at all costs. I came home from school right as my dad backhanded my mom into the wall. As calmly as I could I walked into the kitchen, quietly snuck out the biggest knife I could find, and carefully moved into the bedroom and started jumping on my parent's bed…which my dad absolutely hated…and I knew it."

I shake my head, looking down at the ground. I've never told this story but I feel like Luna needs to know what she's getting into with me, so she can decide if it's too much to bear…to decide if what I did all those years ago scares her, or only serves to reinforce the protector that she sees me as. There can be only one choice, and I'm praying it's the latter.

"As predicted, my dad came storming in to punish me, thunderclouds in his eyes as he spotted me and then rushed at me. But he didn't predict what I was about to do next."

I pause again, reliving the memory in real time for the first time in a long time. I need to just power through it and get it out, get the cathartic release that I need.

"I flew through the air just like the Superman shirt that I had on that day and holding the handle of that knife as tight as my little hands could I drove it straight into my dad's chest... and then hung from it, all my body weight turning the blade inside him as I was just there suspended as he reached for his chest. I was holding a fucking knife buried in my father's chest, hanging on for dear life while I tried to take his, practically the same way most kids would cling to monkey bars when they realize they are in over their heads. That's what I should have been doing at that age, playing at the park. But instead, I was trying to play hero, and in order to be the hero sometimes you have to slay the dragon, even if it's your own flesh and blood."

I look over at the horrified expression Luna has on her face, knowing she sees me as a monster now. Why quit while I'm ahead? Might as well give her the Fully Monty.

"He bled out, but by the time I got back to the room where he'd struck my mom she'd already done the same. The coroner later said she hit the wall awkwardly and in doing so somehow her temple managed to catch a corner. There was nothing the paramedics could do, even though I learned a few hours later that my mom was already trying to do something, which is why the argument that day had escalated so much. Seems my father caught her packing to run away for good. When I went to find her luggage I saw a small backpack next to it...mine, with my matching Superman logo. It was the backpack my mom worked a second job to buy me for my birthday because I liked that damn Superman so much. I just really admired how he protected people, and that's all I ever wanted to do...protect my mom.

"And in her last moments, she was trying to protect me, to get me out of that situation. She'd even called the principal between the time the school day ended and my bus dropped me off, telling him she was pulling me out for the rest of the semester, but I'd be ready to start again next semester.

"It wasn't true. She was just trying not to startle anyone, to buy some time while she got us as far away from my father as she could...but we didn't even manage to get out of the house. If only I hadn't waited. If only I'd protected her a day sooner, a week sooner, a year earlier. But I hadn't. I failed her and failed myself in the process. Never again. That's why I'm a protector. That's why I've dedicated my life to serving and...protecting. And if I haven't scared you enough as it is with this story, that's why you can count on me to protect you...always. I may be a possessive, overbearing asshole part of the time...okay, most of the time."

I pause and we both share a laugh at my candid self-assessment.

"But it's for your own good, your safety, whether you recognize it or not."

Her hand squeezes mine tight and the rest of our food and drinks drop from our laps. I wrap her up in a big hug as the tears roll down her cheeks, pulling her up and onto my lap.

"Are you scared of me now? Think I'm an evil person for what I did to my own flesh and blood?"

She pulls her head from my chest, cupping my face ferociously as she stares right into my eyes. "I think you're amazing," she says and brings her lips to mine.

8

LUNA

I'm not entirely sure if he pulled me into his lap or I climbed into it on my own accord, but regardless that's where I find myself…and I find him already thickening underneath me. He strokes my hair and tips my face up and I get the kiss I so desperately need.

I'm taken aback that he shared such a personal story like that with me, and without me really prodding to get it. I've been my father's daughter for eighteen years and in that time I've barely learned anything about his childhood. With Luke it's so different, the connection so much stronger. The way he encouraged me this morning without saying a word, taking me to the location where I'd like to have a profession one day and then watching out for me while I was there.

He makes me want to take the goals I already have for myself and elevate them. His belief in me only raises my own belief in myself, and I love him for it.

I maneuver, repositioning myself so I'm straddling his much larger body, my foot nowhere close to touching the ground.

As I search for balance I teeter and his thick mitts stabilize me just as I fall forward, my chest pressing into his thick wall of muscle, his two tectonic plates that ripple when my hands reach out to brace my fall, clenching his chest.

"So. Fucking. Mine," he groans, sounding as if his throat is full of sandpaper.

I push up slightly my shorts riding up and part of my bare ass making contact with his pants. Slowly I glide my hips forward, sliding forward and then back in his lap, making sure to hold my position with each movement forward, where I pin his cock to his belly.

First, his eyes roll back and then his head. "Just like that, little girl," he commends, his hands clenching my ass harder, sliding the rest of the way up and underneath my shorts and grasping my globes...hard.

I'm beyond wet, drenched, and I can already feel my moisture seeping through my panties and into my shorts. My hips rifle back and forth, as I drag my hot sex across his manhood, my ass muscles flexing with each increase of pressure of his fingers into my flesh.

"Daddy. What's going on?" I find myself sliding right into 'character' although I'm not playing a game. This is real and my possessive protector is here to make sure whatever happens happens safely. My older man to guide me through this experience.

"Daddy's good little girl is using Daddy to give herself pleasure, honey."

"I—Is that bad?" I wonder aloud.

"No, sweetheart. It's good...very, very good. Just don't stop because Daddy's very pleased too."

I continue working in circles on his lap, feeling a deep, personal place inside me start to quiver. And it's just then I see Reggie off in the distance, looking at us.

"Daddy, somebody's watching."

His eyes go on alert as he scans the area. "I don't like the idea of you coming with all these eyes watching," he raps against my ear.

"Show them all who I belong to, Daddy. Show them what they might be able to see, but can never have. Claim me in front of the world, so everyone knows exactly who I belong to." My boldness shocks me, my words flowing at the same blistering speed of pleasure that concentrates on that place I'm rubbing against his clothed cock, my womanhood clenching. "Everywhere we go I'll be a good girl. I'll sit on your lap and ride you so everyone knows what only Daddy gets to touch, feel, have.

He grunts something feral, animalistic, and way beyond human followed by a hoarse explicative. "Mine," he snarls. "You're right. Let's show them all. Keep rubbing," he demands.

"I can't stop."

"I know how to make you stop. Come. Come for your Daddy."

"Ye—ye—yes, Daddy," I cry out. My back arches like I've been invaded by the same need that's guided me to this same off the charts public display of affection. My hips twist and I feel the dam inside me break, a wall of water rushing inside me as my climax hurtles through me without warning.

My mouth flies open and I feel the need to scream, quickly followed by the need to bite down on something to suppress it. All I can see is the thick, corded muscles coming off his neck and attaching to his shoulder. In this instance they look like ropes of red licorice, the heat coming off him in waves, and I lose my mind as I lose control of my sex in the same breath.

I grab the back of his head and yank my mouth down onto the thick muscle, sinking my teeth into his rough skin causing him to let loose a guttural shout of release that drowns out all the other sounds in the park. I feel his cock jerk underneath me and a hot geyser shoot against the inside of his clothes as my body quakes and unloads on his lap. My muscles curl in on themselves and my teeth sink in deeper into his flesh.

"Oh, Daddy. Thank you, Daddy. Thank you, Daddy."

I'm shaking like I just saw a ghost, my arms vibrating like the coils inside of a toaster, which is exactly how hot I feel. I'm burning up, roasting.

Tapping the underside of my chin with the inside of my index finger which is part of my now clenched fist, my jaw releases and twist my head, my head collapsing into the crook of his neck.

I feel my body elevating, rising, and instinctively I wrap my legs around his waist like a belt as he takes me away, far away from here.

To where, I have no clue, but it doesn't matter…as long as I'm with him.

9

LUKE

Was I disappointed in myself that I was about to claim my best friend's daughter before talking with my lifelong friend about it first? Yes.

Was that about to stop me, or two consenting adults from doing what I brought the only woman that ever mattered to me to this opulent penthouse suite for? Hell, fucking no.

And was I going to take the time and find out why that weirdo from the pool hall was at the amusement park today, seemingly too close the moment Luna rode my lap to completion? Not now. Later.

Right now I was focused on one thing and one thing only.

Making her mine.

The private elevator stops at the top floor, opening into a spacious entryway with high ceilings, marble floors, mirrors, and other decorative embellishments.

The remote to the custom state of the art sound system is practically begging me to try it out, but the only sound I want to hear is the satisfaction I'm about to give to my little girl...all night long.

In the sauna, next to the fireplace, against the floor-to-ceiling windows...all in due time. First I'm going to take her on the four-poster bed on the pristine white Egyptian cotton sheets, just as her first time should be.

Carrying her into the master bedroom I toss her on the bed and move quickly to the private terrace, opening the French doors to allow air to come in. I'm burning up and know it's only going to get hotter.

Advancing back toward the bed, my feet sink into the plush throw rug, but my mind is fixated on my hips sinking as my cock plunges deep into her.

The night air slides over my skin, the city skyline view behind me not even an attraction. How could it be when the most beautiful creature in the universe is right in front of me?

"Was it heavy carrying me all the way here?"

"Stop asking ridiculous questions and start taking off those sexy little clothes that I never should have let you leave the house in," I warn. "And for the record, you're so damn light you'd make a feather seem heavy."

She can't help but smile at that, although my words weren't meant to comfort. They were the truth. Her body slides across the turned down high-quality sheets, satin I think, although I wouldn't know. My existence is Spartan, or at least it was until now. Now it's time to breed her, begin our family, and put everything towards making their life full of the comforts I never knew.

Out of nowhere, I sense that she starts to feel nervous, realizing that she might not please me, might not be enough. Her inexperience is about to be on full display, with nowhere to hide. I hear her swallow, and watch as her face telegraphs the anxiety she's feeling. This isn't the time to let her nervousness or...inexperience...get in the way. She belongs to me. She's mine. And it's time to tell her just how much this means to me, too.

"It's time you learned something else about me," I begin. "Sex isn't something I treat lightly, or at all for that matter. I never wanted to give myself to a woman, or take a part of her, because I knew it wouldn't be all of her...it wouldn't be forever. Just as you don't have experience...well, neither do I. So we're in this together. I'm going to try and hold back and take it slow, but to be honest I don't know how much longer I can wait.

"I've been waiting forty-one years for this moment."

"And I've been waiting the last two riding circles around your house on my bike, just waiting for you to come out and notice me."

"Oh, I noticed you already, but not like this. Not until you were legal. Something happened at your birthday party. I know it and you know it. And since that day alone my body has produced enough come to fill you up a dozen times. I swear I'll try my best not to hurt you getting it all in, although with as tight as you are there's a damn good chance I might need to resort to a little spit and muscle."

She peels down the straps of her tank top, rolling the tight material to her waist so only a bra leaves her covered up top.

"Slower," I growl. I'm the one who told her to take off her clothes but I'm acting more and more like my hands are the ones itching to do the job...like I'm ready to snatch away her panties with an impatient fist. Because that's exactly what I am thirsting to do…with my fist, or my teeth.

She unbuttons her shorts, her little hips wiggling as she slides out of them. How a baby or ten is going to pass through those hips I don't know, but it's going to happen. No, if's, and's, or but's.

Down to her virginal white bra and panties, my hands are practically lurching off my arms to grab her underwear and yank them aside so I can get a peek underneath.

My rod is dripping, rammed up against my goddamn zipper, calling out for my girl's pussy. Surely it's as long as her silky smooth forearm, and nothing is going to stop me from pounding it into her. All of it.

"Keep going. Don't stop," I order, and slowly she unhooks her bra from behind with a shy expression, carefully covering her tits with her hands as the bra falls to the side.

"Show me what I've been waiting my whole life to see." My tone is demanding, and my lips barely move as the words come from somewhere deep in my chest and rumble through my throat.

Her skin is pebbled with goosebumps as she slowly pulls her hands away to reveal two cherry-topped mounds. I move closer, reaching out a hand and tracing the curve of her breasts with my fingertip. "Mine," I intone quietly. "Now the rest."

But before she has the chance, I take the opportunity away from her, my face diving in between her perfect perky breasts as my teeth rake across her skin, my tongue licking the perspiration that dots her cleavage as I continue up and across her collarbone, not biting, just teasing.

I pull back, lightheaded from the vanilla scent that radiates from her, the taste of her skin on my tongue.

"Now be a good girl and finish undressing for Daddy."

As heat blossoms across her skin, she hooks her thumbs inside her panties and slowly slides them down her thighs, her glistening pussy on display. I'm no longer teased by the lines of her lips pressing against the opaque white lacy thong.

"If you only knew all the thoughts rushing through my skull right now. All the debaucherous things fighting to convince me to do them first. To take your clit in my mouth and suck it until you come so hard you explode in my mouth. To flip you over and tongue your puckered hole until it's wet enough for me to slide my dick in. To fist your hair and drag you to me, bringing your warm mouth to my cock while I slide in all my thick inches until you can't breathe until you gag on my massive, throbbing need that you've created...that you're responsible for.

"But that's not how it works. Your pleasure always comes first. And first I have to claim you, making you mine. Put my dick inside you so no man can ever have you. Fill you with my cum until you're so damn full there's no more room. Watch it drip out on the sheets and then fill you up again until sometime next week when you're having lunch or doing some other random life activity you feel my come still seeping from your tight hole.

"How I'm going to breed you. Get you pregnant with our first child and then do it again and again and again until we're one big perfect family, just like how that belly's going to stay...big and happy, filled with my offspring like your pussy will be filled with my seed. Always.

"And I'll never stop. Not even when we have an entire house

full of kids. So you need to be ready, need to understand what you're getting yourself into.

"I know you're young but that doesn't mean you're irresponsible, that you're not an adult, that you can't make a life decision at eighteen that will affect you forever. But I need to hear you say it. Need to know you know just exactly what all this entails. What being mine truly means."

I move in closer, taking her face in my rough hand and not doing it gently either.

"I can't shake this belief that this is why I waited all those years. You. This is fate giving me a chance to be your provider, protector, your lover. Your man. I feel like I've been crawling through the desert for forty-one long, hard grueling years, just looking for a single drop of water. But once I found you it's like that thirst was quenched with a glass of lemonade the size of Niagara Falls. Like you were the answer to everything and in every way.

"There's no going back once we do this. Not a chance in hell, because once I have you if any man so much as even tries to take you from me that's exactly where I'll put him...in the ground so far his soul will be burning until eternity. I protect what's mine and I'm possessive as hell. I'm jealous to a fault, but the good thing about being an obsessed bastard, when it comes to you, is you know you have my full, undivided attention, commitment, and desire. At. All. Times. And that I'll do anything to keep it. Always."

I pause. "Now, if all that sounds good to you let me please you because you know that's how I get off. You don't have to say yes, but you can if you want. All I really need you to tell me is what you think about in the dark, alone in your room at night. Because that's exactly what I'm going to be for you, every night and for always."

"Sex, but not just sex. I mean...I don't exactly know where to start. Not really. Not yet."

"Then let's find that out together. Are you ready for this?"

She nods, and it's not nearly good enough.

"Say it," I groan.

"Say what?"

"Say you're innocent, untried cunt is ready to be spread open wide for me, molding to my cock forever. Tell me you've been a good girl, the best kind of girl. The kind that kept her pussy safe and tight for her first time, for her Daddy."

"All those things are true." She swallows hard and slowly scissors her legs wide open. "It's all for you, Daddy."

Any last bit of control remaining inside me snaps completely. I discard my clothes as quick as humanly possible and launch myself onto the bed like a combative silverback Gorilla, jamming my fists into the mattress as I brace my too big for her body above my princess, as she squirms underneath. I want to pin her down, imprison her, grab her by the throat... but not yet. That will come...in time.

She may be mine but that possessiveness comes with respon-sibilities, such as never hurting her, not recklessness, like not showing the proper care and respect for the gift she's given me...all of her.

I reach down between my thighs, just above the top of my knees as I grab my dick and squeeze until it's so painful I'm sure I've delayed my ejaculation...for now. Her little body underneath me so hot, my anticipation like molten lava, and it's causing me to be on the brink of exploding before I'm even inside her.

Explosive energy shoots through every vein in my body. Violent, masculine needs emanating from every pore in my body.

I'm seconds away from devirginizing my little angel, marking her, claiming her, making her mine forever.

My tongue glides across her body, tasting her like a feral beast that I've become. I'm no longer a man, and the only thing that can quench this thirst inside me is the relief of unloading this special seed inside her, breeding her forever, making her belly grow with my firstborn child.

Our firstborn child.

Nothing can calm this need, can quiet these voices of the sound of a little person, human life, calling me 'dad', just like the sound of her calling me Daddy plays over and over again in my mind like a broken record.

"Mine," I growl into her flesh. "My life and mine to fuck, to claim, to fill with my cock."

"Yes," she whimpers. "Yours."

Lining the crown of my cock up to her opening, I run it up and down through her folds, coating it with her musky stickiness. One pass and I'm lubricated enough that I just might fit inside her, although I still have to be safe. I will not hurt her. Ever.

"I like the way that feels," she whimpers. "I didn't know…"

"You better not know," I growl.

"It's all so new to me."

"And me too. But no more waiting." I bring my forehead to hers, staring into her eyes so deep I swear I can see her soul. "You ready for this, because I can't hold on much longer. Once I'm inside that perfect body of yours there's no going back."

"I'm ready," she confirms.

And with her blessing, my hips relax and I slide inside her, my dick slides into her, coming to a rest as it snaps into place, her pussy locking me in place as if it's the final piece of a jigsaw puzzle I've been working on my entire life, yet never knew I was. Like it was always happening in the background and my life, despite seemingly good on the outside, was always missing something on the inside. Some little thing gnawing at me.

That's gone now. Everything's melted away into the background. A completeness fills me, as I fill her with my throbbing flesh.

"You okay?"

She nods. "I want you to fuck me, Luke. Fuck me just like you've dreamed of."

"I might hurt you."

"You won't. Don't hold back. I want to feel your power, see your need, experience this transformation I'm seeing in you. I want it all, and I want it now."

Her demand catches me off guard, but I waste no time in obliging her, and me in the process.

Slowly I slide out of her and then back in, stretching her flesh. "That's it, baby girl. Take it deep for Daddy, little one," I encourage as I push deeper inside.

"Yes," she manages on an exhale. "Yes, Daddy."

I slowly start to work my hips before the last of my control leaves me, evaporating into thin air. My hands grab her hips violently as I thrust into her. One of her hands shoots up to her midsection as if there's a knifing pain in her middle. Before I can ask her if she's okay, she reads my expression.

"Don't stop. It's perfect."

It's then I realize her hand is over her stomach in a way that signals she's not in pain. It's more of an uncomfortable full session, and her nerve endings between her legs are probably screaming.

She's close to screaming out in ecstasy. That's what I have to wait for before I can roar my damn self.

Her legs scramble on the mattress, her hips shifting and then flexing, her ass coming off the sheets and then back down, as if she's trying to accommodate, to find a more comfortable way to endure my hulking member which is impaling her as my hands hold her in place.

There's no escaping me, little girl. Not now. Not ever. I'm in it to win it, and winning can only be defined in one way. A big, happy family and us together...forever.

Out of nowhere, I moan so loud it hurts my own eardrums. The corded muscles of my forearms ripple, then shake, my chest muscles flexing and I know I'm too damn close to unloading.

Must please her first or I'll never forgive myself, I recite inside my head like a damn caveman.

The memory foam beneath us starts making a noise almost as if it were squeaking like a box spring. The headboard of the bed rebounds off the wall and I thrust back into her, the headboard now moving in a vicious circle with the rhythm of our bodies.

My balls feel like they're being strangled, and I try my damnedest to keep from spilling as I continue tearing into the most beautiful woman this universe has ever seen. My woman.

The feet of the bed scrape back and forth against the floor as I ride her hard. Every part of the room feels like it's groaning under the weight of the invisible elephant in the room…my need to get her to climax while I'm buried to the hilt inside her.

Her head springs forward and back, her damp hair flopping every which way as her body covers in sweat, liquid heat molding her cunt to my throbbing bulge.

A possessive roar leaves my lungs, causing the oversized windows to shake and the front legs of the bed to give out, the wood splintering as my body lurches forward as her perfection is now at a new angle, her hips tilted up so I can get even deeper.

I jerk Luna up and into me, thrusting her body onto my cock. One hand leaves her midsection as I cup her head into the crook of my neck, protecting her.

"It feels so good, Daddy." Her teeth chatter into my skin. "Don't. You. Stop."

"Can't stop. Won't stop. Never," I grunt. "I couldn't pull my cock out of you if this fucking building was on fire.

My back goes ramrod straight, my abs clenching as I sense my eruption approaching.

She tries to wrap her legs around my back, but I'm taking her too aggressively and she can't clench down. Every thrust of my cock shakes her legs loose. I'm giving her everything and I'm ready to give her that final thing…but not until she gives me hers…first.

Then it hits me what my little girl needs and I immediately give it to her.

My permission.

"Daddy needs you to come, little girl."

"I'm close. I just…c—c—can't."

"You can and you will. On three your tight little pussy is going to come for Daddy, squeeze his cock tight and milk him of all his seed. You understand me?"

"But, Da—"

"No butts. You will. Now…three, two…one," I count down quickly giving her mind no time to think. "Come for Daddy, sugar. Come for him now!"

"Ut…uh." Her fingers curl into the sheets as if holding onto them is going to save her. "Oh my God. Here it comes!"

Her climax hurtles through her, her body lurching toward me as her nails rake down my back. "Daddy, so good. So fucking good."

A prideful roar from deep within my belly comes tumbling out of me, but I don't tip my head back like my subconscious so demands. No, I keep my eyes focused right on her, staring into those baby blues as she has an orgasm while looking right at me, while my dick is buried to the hilt inside her tight little pussy, which is completely seized up and coating me in her sweetness.

And that sight and the feeling of her getting what she needs is the sound of the gun being fired at the beginning of an Olympic sprint, and my seed explodes out of me in a race to be the lucky one to coat her womb, to impregnate her, to bond her to me forever as we become a family once and for all.

All these forty-one years and I've never felt anything like this. Nothing even compares. Because nothing compares to her, to us, to how we'll forever be bonded.

After the aftershocks start to die out or bodies collapse onto the bed together. We laugh, having forgotten the bed's no longer level.

But we don't care. We've got each other and that's all that matters…now, tomorrow, always.

10

LUNA

The next morning

I watch from the bed as Luke's towel falls from his waist to the floor as he rounds the corner from the bathroom to shower.

Pulling the down comforter up to my neck I melt into the mattress.

I can't help but smile, thinking of how books have always been such a big part of my life and now Luke's even used a few from the room to prop the broken end of the bed back up. When I suggested we just tell the hotel and take another room, he looked at me like I was crazy, telling me that he wasn't about to allow anyone to come inside the room. The night was ours, and the memory, the visuals...even including the room, would be shared by no one.

The man is possessive, there's no doubt about it.

But just as he's possessive about me and my body, he's also possessive about taking the strain of day to day living from my mind and handling it all on his own. I should be worried about moving out, paying taxes, and being responsible for myself. Talk about a step up from just worrying about passing a simple high school exam.

Luke isn't having any of that. When I asked him in the middle of the night what he has planned he told me not to worry my pretty little head about it, his words exactly. That he's got it all figured out and all taken care of. The craziest part is that I trust him enough to just allow him to fold his protective wings around me and take that responsibility, that burden off my plate.

I'm so used to boys my age who sit back and do nothing, and who have no backbone. Most 'guys' these days are just as bad as reality show women when it comes to gossip and criticizing. He has no time, energy, or desire for that. I would say he's focused on solving problems, but with him, there never seem to be problems. He's always got them solved before they even become issues, although I've certainly created one for him when it comes to his current employment situation.

He promised me that it's nothing, that it will pass, or if not he can always get a job in a new city. He shrugs it off as if it doesn't even matter, all the while I'm pretty sure this penthouse suite isn't exactly something a man on a police officer's salary could afford for more than a night or two.

I used to think a guy who tried to force all his decisions on you would be more of something along the lines of a macho douchebag. But now the fantasy, the reality, of Luke is just too enticing...too much to really believe. The most incredible part is that he's not so dominating that he won't let me think for myself, and even encourages my dream of being a crime reporter.

I expected to be an insignificant cog in the churning wheel of a newsroom, but no...he already saw to it that I have someone watching over me, that everyone knows they can't take advantage of me. And I feel like he's put me in the front of the line, to make sure I get a position where I can realize my dream sooner than not.

This is *nothing* like I've ever experienced before, but exactly what I've always wanted. Just as I've always wanted him.

My possessive policeman steps into the doorway, rubbing a new towel against his hair as he stands there, nude for me to admire as he finishes drying off.

"Did I make you angry when I went to that crime scene?" I question aloud.

"Sweetheart," he says, taking quick steps toward me before cupping my chin with his index finger and thumb. "There is nothing you can ever say or do, nothing in this world, that would make me feel anything but...good thing about you."

Was that pregnant pause almost the word...love?

I swallow hard and prepare myself to change the subject. I don't want to get into a rush. I know he's saying this is forever, and I know he's a man of his word, but my father has let me down more times than I can count, or care to remember. So I'm not about to get my hopes up too high...yet.

"What's the plan for today?"

"I go downtown to do some work. You stay here and don't leave the room."

"Like your sex slave? Your kept woman."

"I'm not joking around here, little one." His tone turns very serious, and my back straightens as I scramble a bit back on the bed.

"But how can you work. You're suspended, right?"

"Officially...yes. Unofficially...I've been with the force enough years and know enough people to still do a thing or two out there and figure out who in the hell is terrorizing our town."

"You're going to try and catch the kidnapper?"

"I'm not going to try. I am."

"But what about me?" It's selfish and I realize it just as soon as the words slide from my tongue, but it's too late to take them back.

"This is all about you, about us. I'm not about to bring a child into this world in an unsafe place. I am bringing a child into this world. That's a foregone conclusion and although I'm not a gambling man, I'd bet good money you're already pregnant with our first."

"Luke!"

"In my eyes, it wouldn't even be gambling. I'm sure there's a life growing inside you, just as we both want. And I'm going to clean up the streets swiftly, now so any evildoers know that this town is protected by me. And I don't fuck around. I keep our streets safe for my family and the families of my neighbors."

"Isn't it dangerous to go about this while you're suspended?"

"It's more dangerous, more damaging, to think that someone even considers the fact that they can come to our town and threaten to disrupt the safe environment I've spent a lifetime solidifying. People in this town have rested easy for years knowing I've got it taken care of. That's being tested and when a man is tested he has three options. Freeze, flight, or fight. And you know for damn sure which one I'm choosing."

As if it was ever a question.

"I should go home then. This room must cost—"

"A small pittance to know that you're locked up in here in a Fort Knox in the sky with security guards at the door and elevators that don't function without room keys. Not to mention no other room key goes to our suite so no one can come up here unless we request their presence...which you won't."

He's getting a bit bossy now, but I realize it's for my own good. He doesn't have time to consult me or ask me if he would even consider that in the first place. Doubtful.

But I have no doubts he has my best interests in mind, even though he's going about it in a bit of a cavemanish way. This is the part of the handing over the decision making that I'm going to have to get used to because there's no way he's going to budge on things like this.

"Luke, I feel guilty about sitting here all day in this expensive—"

"And how guilty would I feel if something happened to you because I was too cheap to spend what amounts to nothing when compared to all the money I've saved over a lifetime? It's no secret that police work is my life. I never spend money on vacations or fancy things. I don't have time for starters, nor do I have the need. So if I can invest a very, very small fraction of that money, and it is an investment by the way, in your security...then I'm doing that every single time."

"Investment in my security. My dad has cameras on the outside of the house, a system that—"

"No more." He puts his foot down, literally, and my mouth snaps shut...but strangely my pussy feels like it's slowly opening, begging this possessive man who's actually on the borderline of being a dickhead, to slide right back into me. I don't know what's racking my brain more...that I'm allowing him to be this way, or that I'm actually secretly enjoying it.

"I'll be back before dinner, and will call to check in with you throughout the day."

I nod.

"Just stay put."

"What about food? Can I at least order delivery?"

"The fridge is stocked with sandwiches, desserts, and every drink under the sun. I even saw some Capri Sun packets in there." He pauses. "Thought you might like them for some reason."

"You thought right." He's moved away from the bed to get dressed, and I look at him over the top of the covers, only my eyes and the top of my head revealed.

"That's even better."

"What's better?"

"Just stay in bed, completely covered all day."

"Why is that better?"

"No one can see you through the windows and you can rest. You're going to need your sleep for what I have planned for later."

"Which might be?"

"There's no 'might' to it. It's what will be. And you'll see. Later."

He moves back to me, kissing me softly on the forehead as he cups the softcover around my face.

"Don't open the door for anybody."

"Not even you?" I tease.

"You won't have to open it for me because my need for you will have me putting a boot into it, destroying it to get to you."

"So I'll hear you coming."

"Oh, you'll hear me coming all right, in more ways than one."

"Luke!" I toss a pillow at him, but he just bends slightly at the waist, dodging it as if there was never even a snowball's chance in the desert that it might actually hit him, even though it was a perfect throw destined to do exactly that.

Luke is my destiny, it's clear. But can I really put up with his bossiness, his possessiveness?

I know I can, but I need to think long term. Will this eventually turn into Chinese water torture or death by a thousand cuts?

He gives me a wink and slides out the door.

No. It won't turn into that, because he'd never hurt me. He's doing this all to protect me. Because he cares so much... something I can't say about any other man I've ever met.

And that's exactly why I should make him some brownies for later tonight. It will give me something to do today, and a way to say thank you for everything he's already done. Not to mention, whoever needed an excuse for brownies? Not me, that's for sure.

But it might serve as another excuse...to get me out of the suite. I have a pretty good idea of what area he's going to be working in. And if I can get these made in the next hour or two, I can go down there mid-day, while the sun is out and there are plenty of people on the street.

What's the worst that could happen? Sure, he might get angry at me, but seeing his face and him seeing mine should cure that. And if not, then I guess he'll just have to spank me...later.

He thinks he has everything planned out for tonight, but I need to remind him I have plans of my own.

This is a two-way street after all. Even if he's going to be possessive to the point of testing how much of his over-bearing nature I can take...well, then...it's better he knows now that I'm capable of pushing back from time to time.

A little push pull, as the saying goes. And maybe it will lead him to push me onto the bed, or pulling me over his knee.

Either way, we both win.

I move quickly toward the kitchen and confirm that there aren't enough ingredients on hand.

I'll just jump in the shower real quick and request the ingredients from the kitchen. They should be able to bring them up. Sure, I could probably buy some from room service, but it wouldn't be the same.

I need to put my heart into making these. He's already got my beating lifeblood in his hands. Now just to get cleaned up, make this dessert, and show him that nothing can keep us apart. Even if he did make it crystal clear that I wasn't to leave.

But I'm going to be by his side, so it isn't really leaving. It's bringing us back together.

I miss him already, and I sure don't miss sitting around in my room all day at home. And I can't repeat that same thing here.

I need to be by his side, to feel that energy, that protectiveness, that sense of completion that he gives me...even if he goes about it in his own original way.

His way or the highway, I guess. He can be my Frank Sinatra with his 'my way' mantra. I'll gladly be his Marilyn Monroe, and we can live the charmed life...together.

11

LUNA

An hour and a half later I'm filled with curiosity as I tuck the tray of brownies into my backpack and with my head tilted down I begin my walk down the streets in the city center. A slow smile builds across my face as I contemplate Luke's potential questions as to why I left the hotel.

Because I want to surprise my man. I'm expecting him to call anytime now and when he does I'll simply ask him where he is and go there if I haven't found him already. But I'd definitely prefer to surprise him, see that look on his face, and feel that sense of surprise fill me when I see him go from angry to excited to see his girl.

I grow more and more eager as I continue searching. There's a spring in my step and when I catch sight of my eyes in a reflection in a shop window, there's a glow to them.

I lick my lips and smile, blowing out a long breath. Where is he?

It's taken me longer to find him than I thought. My dad once told me this is the three block radius where he likes to do most of his detective work. I just wonder why I haven't seen him here now. Doubt creeps in, and I start to wonder if I'm going to find him at all before he calls. My movement becomes short and jerky, and I catch myself pacing more than walking.

Haven't I already been down this street? My backpack almost slides off my shoulder and I laugh at my clumsiness.

I bite down on my lip, eagerness the emotion that wins out again, my fears starting to melt away like chocolate in the sun on a summer day.

I just hope I don't disappoint him, or that my food does either.

It's in that moment I realize I'm obsessed with him, even more than I already figured. I long to hear the pitch of his deep voice, his laser-focused gaze locked on me and that worry that he'll exhibit when he sees me out of the penthouse suite, even though I know I'm fine and nothing's going to happen to me, especially in such a short time in the middle of the day.

My own eyes narrow and I spot a man leaning against a brick wall adjacent to a barbershop. I bounce from one foot to the other, trying to control the squealing, hooting, and hollering that's going on inside me.

Found ya!

I fan myself, trying to cool my rapidly increasing body temperature so I can approach him with cheeks less red than the crimson hue they've just taken in the last few seconds.

The effect this man has on me. Unbelievable, and I can't believe he's mine all mine.

Or is he?

I feel my body go weightless and everything starts to spin. I take a step back and my eyes widen and then bulge. Another step back and my mouth hangs open as my body completely freezes.

I'm blinking uncontrollably as I try to process what I'm seeing.

My palm comes up to my mouth, covering it and I quickly turn my head away and duck into an alley.

I need to sit down before I pass out. My back finds the wall and I slide down it into a heap.

Stunned isn't even the word. My shoulder slouch and my arms hang loosely at my sides as my recently bright eyes go dull...I'm sure of it.

Every muscle in my face goes slack as I just sit there, limply.

Confusion fills me and I start swallowing, trying to clear my throat and get some air at the same time, failing miserably.

"How could this be?" I repeat over and over again under my breath, my words trailing off at the end of each sentence.

It can't be. That's the answer. I must be mistaken.

There's no way I saw what I thought I saw. It can't be him, not like that.

I cross my arms and muster the energy to stand, adjusting my backpack and peeking out from around the corner of the alley.

My hand raises to my breastbone and then falls back down to my side.

No, it's him. It's Luke and he's chatting up what most certainly looks to be a woman of the night, in the middle of the day. The worst part, the part that hurts the most, is that she looks somewhat like me. And this from the man that said that I resembled no one, only to reveal, in what he thought was secrecy, that he indeed does have a type.

Am I special like he made me feel? Clearly not.

And when he stuffs his hand in his pants and pulls out a wad of cash, handing it to the girl, and then she motions for him to give her more, the tears start to fall.

He obliges and then they both slide around the corner and disappear...together.

I want to do the same. I wish I was an ostrich so I could bury my head in the sand, never to see again.

Sweat covers my skin as my chin dips, my chest caves, and my spine bends in embarrassment.

I wince, wondering how I set myself up for such pain.

He protected me because he's my dad's best friend. But then he realized it was wrong, but he'd gone too far. He was emotional from losing his job, or at least being indefinitely suspended from it, and took refuge...inside of me.

But now I'm seeing another side of him. As a boy in blue, even if he doesn't wear the uniform as he works undercover, he has access to loads of women. They must be throwing themselves at him.

But why would he pay for sex?

And why would he tell me he was a virgin, just like me?

Maybe I'm nothing more than a person of interest now and

he's working me over, just like some of the crime books I've read. I was at the crime scene after all and upset everyone by being there.

Strangely, it's clear now that he's using an old reporter's trick on the girl who wants to be a reporter. Seduce and betray.

I was already seduced before I got to him. He's always been the one and only for me. All he had to do was give me what I want, tell me what I want to hear, and then betray me when the time was right.

But in his mind, he hasn't even betrayed me yet, because he doesn't know what I know.

Maybe I am just a young, naive girl. I jam my hands in my coat pocket, wondering why I feel so inadequate yet again. It's always been that way for my father and now it's equally as bad for his best friend.

Is it just bad luck or am I not...enough?

Either way, I'm humiliated. My breath hitches as the crying continues. I make myself as small as possible, trying to shield my body from what, I'm not exactly sure. The world I guess. The hope it had given me and then was snatched away just as quickly.

My bottom lip trembles and my chin along with it as I catch myself whimpering.

"What does she have that I don't?" I utter in between deep inhales, my body searching for air.

I want to tear out of here, grab her, and punch her in the face. And I'm not even a violent person, although you'd never guess that from my clenched teeth and the ugly laughter that's rolling out of me in waves.

"Bitch," I mutter under my breath, resorting to name calling now.

Unappreciated. Powerless. Vulnerable. Worthlessness. All feelings I've tried to get away from, feelings that Luke had made a distant memory, only for the same person to make them come storming back.

And now I just want to slide out of here quietly, forget this ever happened. The worst part is I envy what that paid escort, or whatever the word for her profession, has that I don't. But I can't make a man love me. I've already come to accept that thanks to my father.

No amount of despair, anguish, or hurt will fix that.

At this point, I'm not even appalled or angry. This is just the reality of the way things are. Betrayal is real, bitterness is imminent. And I regret that I ever dreamt up this idea that I could get the man that I wanted, and put myself, and my heart, out there in his hands, under his care.

It's disgusting really, and my contempt for myself has a bitter taste forming in my mouth right now.

My dreams have been dashed in a single moment, the devastation real. Sure, I'll go home and go through a hysterical crying phase. It will probably last a day or two, but at least it will happen alone, where I'll vow to never let another man hurt me ever again.

"Screw him," I mumble. "How dare he think he could tell me when I could and couldn't leave the suite, how to dress, and how he had the gall to try and make all the decisions in life for me. Who in the hell does he think he is, anyway?"

"Maybe he was just the wrong guy for the job," a strange voice says from behind me.

Am I hallucinating?

"Because I'm going to lock you up better than he ever did and dress you up just like the doll that you are. And you're going to love it, aren't you, little girl? How nice. He already started to break you in."

An evil laugh cuts through the air, but as I go to jump to my feet and spin a forearm wraps around my waist, and a cloth is pressed into my face.

I try and bite down on the hand underneath the rag, to kick and scream, but whatever's on that rag is too strong, as is the man who has me.

Maybe this is my actual destiny, a little girl only to be done in by possessive older men who make me think they have my interests in mind but in reality, are only self-serving.

It's the last thing that goes through my mind before everything goes dark.

12

LUKE

I slam the door shut to the unisex bathroom we've just entered, located on the side of the gas station.

"Tell me what you saw. Exactly," I growl at Detective Aimee Johnson, who I've worked with for years, and who today is undercover as a prostitute, and just messaged me in code, telling me to meet her as soon as I could.

"A John," she begins, using the common term for any man who solicits prostitutes, "or at least I thought he was. I'd never seen him before. He came asking for a specific type of girl," she says hastily. "I thought he was messing with me, trying to be cheeky or something because he was describing me in a lot of ways. I thought it was a slam dunk, and we'd have him cuffed and at the station within ten minutes. Case closed. So I played along, knowing he was going to agree to trade sex for money, but I didn't want to jump the gun. Let the process play out so the charge sticks." She pauses and I tap my toe.

"I know how it works. What. Happened?" I annunciate, putting my hand on the wall and leaning in closer to her.

"I told him he found what he was looking for, that I was it. He looked me up and down and I raised my hand to my wig, ready to tap the call button hidden underneath for backup to come in and make the bust, knowing the takedown was imminent. Then he surprised me. In a very calculated way, he said I 'wasn't quite it.' He wanted something more like 'that girl on TV that the cop got busted for taking out of the station the other day. The one that was on the news that had been found out by the forest.'"

"And then?" I need this information yesterday. Just the thought that someone might be targeting my Luna has my blood boiling.

"I told him not to worry, that I'd be all he wanted and more, opening my top a little bit more. But then he said he wasn't looking to pay for sex. He was interested in…other things. Real creepy guy, right?"

"He referred to the location as the forest and not the crime scene?"

"I picked up on that too," she confirms, nodding and confirming he doesn't see it as a crime scene because he doesn't see what he did there as a crime…if in fact, it was him which it's quickly shaping up to point in that direction.

"Did you follow him?"

"How? I'm working the corner."

"Tell me you put someone on him."

She just shakes her head. "We had nothing on him."

"You should have called me right away and you know it."

"And blow the cover I've worked years building because of a hunch you have?"

"We both have it. It's why you did call me."

"Detective." She puts a finger in my chest. "Need I remind you that there were two other officers in the car watching me. Officers that are still in the car, in that same spot, watching me. I'm risking a lot just coming over here. You know how hard it is to convince the other officers I'm taking a quick bathroom break and to make it look like to the other side of the street I'm actually turning tricks? Not to mention if anyone on the street knows who you really are. I could be in deep shit, *officer*. Oh, wait. You're suspended so I'm taking on even more risk just by being here with you and talking to you about police work. And I had to slide inside the gas station and buy a preloaded burner phone because there's no way the station isn't surveilling your calls. *Now* you can either thank me or beat it."

"I'm going to do both. Thank you. I didn't mean to snap at you it's just…"

"I know. You don't have to say. I've never seen you like this before so I know she's special."

"And thankfully safe, at a location that should be pretty bulletproof for the few hours I needed to get out and see what I could find out." I pause. "You see where that guy went?"

"No, but there's surveillance on that side of the building so I can try and pull footage later tonight, or figure out a way to alert someone, and tell them this might be connected."

"Do it, Aimee. Don't waste another second."

"I know. I just have to be careful, and you know we're getting closer to taking down a big player here today. We're hoping we might get him this time. Slippery bastard. He seems to always be a step ahead of us."

"I'll let you get back to it." I pause. "And thank you. She does mean the world to me and I won't forget the risk you took to keep her safe."

"I'll remember that the next time there's one donut in the box and you're eyeing it like a starving animal."

"It's yours, and all the donuts you want into eternity. I just want my streets safe, especially now that I have something," I pause, clearing my throat, "someone, who means so much to me and who's counting on me for so much."

"Go out there and track this bastard down then."

"That's exactly what I'm going to do, right after I confirm she's okay. Thanks, Aimee."

We exchange fist bumps and Aimee slides out of the bathroom, just as a normally paid sex session in a public bathroom might go down. I use the quick second alone to hit the one on my phone, already having programmed in Luna's number as my top priority speed dial.

And...no answer.

Quickly, I open the GPS app on her phone and it shows that...she's here? What the...

I follow the app, being careful not to get in the line of sight of the team Aimee is working with. I don't want to put her in danger with the boys at the station, especially not wanting them to think she's feeding me information on the exact case I got kicked off of.

Darting into the alley, maintaining the smallest profile I can, yet failing miserably, I see the blue dot indicating my location on the GPS app sitting right on top of hers. This makes no sense.

Quickly I call the front desk of the hotel, demanding in no uncertain terms they send someone up, specifically a woman, to the room to check on her. I want to put my fist through the wall. My stomach is in my throat as I pace, waiting for the damn hold music to go away so I get the answer that I want. That she's there and somehow I picked up her phone by accident, in addition to mine, and it slipped out of my pocket when I came by in this direction in order to meet up with the undercover detective...although I didn't really walk this close to the alley did I? I was a good few feet away. It doesn't really make—

"Sir. She's not there."

"You're sure? You checked everywhere?"

"Everywhere," the woman replies with confidence.

I end the call, my mind racing, all manners out the window. I need to stay calm, fall back on my training, and remain logical.

Why in the hell would she not be in the room and her phone here, close to where I am. This makes absolutely no sense.

"Think, Luke. Think."

I run faster than I ever have to my car, firing up the engine and letting the whole neighborhood know I'm leaving.

I floor it, tires spinning and smoking before they bite down on the hard concrete as I gun it to the one place that I have to go to figure this out fast.

And the one place I'm strictly barred from entering.

13

LUKE

I slam my palm into the police station front door, the wall shaking as the door flies open, ricocheting off it, the doorstop breaking.

The desk sergeant stands. "Detective, I mean Luke. I'm instructed not to let you pass."

If he wasn't behind bulletproof glass I'd grab him by the neck and take the key myself.

"A girl's life is in danger!" I shout. Protocol be damned. We need to do what's right.

The desk sergeant purses his lips, knowing he should open that door but doesn't.

"You open that fucking door right now or I'm going to find a way to bust through it." My nostrils flare, the muscles in my neck corded. Spittle builds up in the corners of my mouth as I plant my feet wide apart.

"What's going on, Luke?" another sergeant who must have heard from the back asks, coming to the entryway.

"I need in, now. We've got a possible abduction. Don't you see? We're losing time. Every minute in a kidnapping multiplies the chances of…"

I can't even think about it. The thought that something happened to my little Luna is beyond devastating. "Open the fucking door!" a guttural demand leaves me yet again.

"Just give me the information and I'll run it through the system."

I look at the metal legs of the chair next to me, knowing that no matter how hard I slam them against that damn bulletproof glass it won't break. But then I catch a break.

An officer with his head down, whistling of all things, passes through the outer door. Not wasting a single second, not thinking, I grab him in a headlock and push him back into the middle ground area…no man's land where you're locked in a plastic box between entering and leaving, similar to how a high-end jewelry store buzzes you through a front door, and then you're in a holding area before they buzz you into the actual showroom.

"Let me in or I'll choke him out," I demand, my threat muffled by the thick glass.

"Can't do it."

"Let…" the officer chokes, his hand reaching for the glass, fingers scraping down.

"Sorry, Jeff," I mumble into his ear.

The second sergeant behind the desk mouths, 'let him in,' to the desk sergeant and the entry door flies open.

I carefully guide Jeff down to the floor and then take off toward the surveillance area.

"Stop!" someone yells as I hurdle a desk, energy shooting through me as I bust my way toward the desk of our IT guy who's got a seemingly unlimited supply of cameras around the city on live feed.

"Pull up the camera where Aimee's working today."

"What? I…"

"Do it now!" I order.

"Hands on your head and down to the ground," someone yells as I hear a gun cock behind me.

I know they won't shoot, and even if they do I don't care. A life without Luna isn't a life worth living. And if some prick is doing something…bile rises in my mouth. If she's in danger and I don't take every possible step necessary to end it, I could never live with myself again.

I turn, my eyes bloodshot red and my skin an even darker shade of crimson. "Back the fuck up," I order the rookie cop whose hands are trembling. "And watch how a real man serves and protects his flock."

"This one?" the IT kid asks, and my head jerks around so quickly it would make Linda Blair's character in *Poltergeist* jealous.

"Back up the footage. Look for a guy trying to solicit."

My entire body is shaking. The kid can't hit the buttons fast enough.

"There! Freeze it! Zoom."

The boy does as he's told and as the face becomes larger and larger on the screen I instantly recognize him. The guy from the pool hall, the tattoo visible from the elevated angle of the camera which has a view down his shirt.

"Fast forward."

I watch, my heart dropping as the IT kid flips through different cameras as we follow him...until he sneaks up on my Luna and chloroforms her. Every ounce of life falls out of my body as I watch him pull her into a van, and then a bolt of electricity shoots through me.

"Follow the van," I order, but it's the obvious thing to do and the kid's already on it.

"You're suspended. Get him out of here!" a voice calls out.

I grip the table hard as I hear the sound of boots coming my way.

"I can't give you any more," the kid says. "I could lose my job."

"You're going to lose the ability to eat solid food when I break your fucking jaw if you don't shut up and get me what I need in the next five seconds."

I turn to face the oncoming mob of police officers, looking back over my shoulder at the screen, watching the van drive out toward the old state road.

"There's nothing that way for miles."

"Is my access revoked?" I ask under my breath.

The kid nods.

"You enable it right fucking now or you'll never get out from behind this desk."

He hits a few keys and I jump up on his desk and dart for the back door. Tapping my keycard to the reader by the door it flashes red…and then green.

I push through, running to the fleet of police cars lined up, knowing there's no way I can get out front to my Mustang. The other officers will take me down out there.

I jerk open the door of the car closest to the exit, the motor pool officer yelling at me as the other officer who's checking out the car runs in my direction.

Too late. I hit the red and blue's and the siren wails as I peel out of the lot. Stuffing my hand into my pocket I yank out my phone and call up Red, a salty old cop who's been giving out speeding tickets in the next town over for longer than I've been alive.

"Red," I ask frantically as he picks up on the fifth ring.

"At your service, Luke."

"You see a white van come through today?"

"Nope. Been sitting here all day too. Nothing that fits that description."

I look in the rearview expecting to see pursuing cars any second now. Contemplating asking Red to send over backup from his city, I finally decide against it. Where I'm going is right on the county line. I know the place because I used to hide there as a kid out by the old state road, trying to do anything to get a few minutes of reprieve from my father and the demon he was.

How ironic, because now that sanctuary is where I'm going to send the prick that kidnapped Luna straight to hell. I'm going to put him there all right, and I don't need a bunch of other officers to witness it. My mind is already set on what

I've got to do, but I can't go to jail. Not because I'd be surrounded by all the bad guys I've put away over the years, who would do their best to make short work of me if I spent a single second in the general population...but because I wouldn't be able to be on the outside, to protect what's mine. Her.

As I clear the city limits I put the pedal all the way to the floorboard, the police car catching air on a bump. I kill the lights and the noise, knowing I need to come in under the radar to make this work.

And I will because my woman's life is in danger. I've been serving and protecting for half my life, but that all serves as stage practice for the rescue I need to do now. *This* is the one that matters because it's her. And she's everything.

14

LUNA

A haze of disorientation covers me like a warm blanket. I feel wetness on my face and look up to see a cavernous structure above me.

I try and scream, but my mouth is covered in tape. There's a flashlight shining in my face and I can't open my eyes all the way, pain pounding in my skull.

"Ahhh, so you've decided to join us," ripping the tape from my mouth.

The light cuts and I look up to see a...man with a wig that looks like a mop of curly red hair and a red dress. "Leapin' lizards!" he says, leaning in to inspect me, causing me to jerk away as best I can, and alerting me to the fact that I'm hand-cuffed. "Look who came for the tea party, Sandy," he says addressing a stuffed animal dog.

I look to my right and left, my body filled with fear as I try and make out the blurry shapes and colors surrounding me. The fog of confusion that circled me was as thick as the actual haze the lights in this dingy, dark, dank place tried to cut through.

I close my eyes and moan, cursing this day. I should have just listened and stayed in the suite. I should have never trusted Luke. And doing so just got me here, on my knees in front of a clearly deranged man.

"A new doll to play with," he says. My eyes open and I hear cries coming from either side of me. I focus as hard as I can and see there are other girls down here too. My entire body covers in goosebumps as I look at their emaciated forms, clearly not being fed enough, and the lifelessness in their eyes.

How long have they been down here?

What has he done to them?

What does he have planned for me?

"Would you like some tea?" he asks, clapping his hands together and rushing off before coming back with a tea set. "Don't worry. Your cop friend won't be coming to spoil our party. He'll never find you here. No one will, so we can have tea, interrupted, each and every day." He pauses, before sweeping his hand out to either side. "Look. I even invited some friends!"

I can't do it, looking down at the ground and unable to take in the sight of the other girls. There must be three or four others and it looks like they've already resigned themselves to whatever fate this is.

"Look at the tea I prepared," he says. "Look at it!" he orders, his hand coming across my face when I refuse to raise my head.

Once I do a grin the size of the Cheshire Cat's spreads across his face. "There now. Be a good girl and mind your manners."

He steps back, making a tsking sound as if he's disappointed in the way I'm acting down in this dungeon.

"I'm sorry I hit you, friend. It's just that...you were snooping around at the same place where I found our friend Jennifer," a moan from one of the other girls is audible, quite possibly from hearing her own name, "and I've been in a grouchy mood ever since. I knew that meant you wanted to come join us, but I wasn't able to get you here sooner." He pauses, his mood changing on a dime. "But now you're here!" He claps his hands together again and the waterworks start streaming down my cheeks.

"Don't cry. That only makes me hard."

I'm so confused I don't know what to think. He's dressed up like Orphan Annie, a girl, but he sticks a hand up underneath his dress and touches himself, clearly knowing he's a man.

"And when I get hard I need relief that only a little girl like you can provide."

My head falls again as if the string that was holding it up had been cut.

His hand comes across my face for a second time and my jaw jerks to the side, my knees dragging across the rough rock on the dirt beneath me as I see a mouse crawling inches from my bare feet.

"Help!" I yell, the sound of my own voice echoing multiple times.

He lunges forward, trying to slap the tape back across my mouth.

"You open your mouth like that and no tea for you, bitch."

Cocking his hand I pull my body away, squinting as I prepare for the blow.

"You never put your hands on a woman," a guttural voice echoes through this cold, stale place, must and mildew smells wafting every which way.

There's a loud thud and the slap never comes, the man falling backward and a rock rolling to the side.

The sound of boots on the rock underneath me drowns out the sound of the flap of bat wings and the squeaks of small animals skittering about.

I hear the sound of choking and look up to see Luke gripping my kidnapper by the neck. Luke puts a forearm to his face multiple times, his lips, mouth, and nose quickly covered in blood, his face as red as the dress he's wearing.

"You motherfucker," Luke spits. "I'm going to make you pay for everything you've done. I'm going to break you in half and then break the halves in half again. I'm going to take my fucking time with you, make it hurt."

Through the darkness, Luke looks enraged, savage, and nothing like the man I know. It was clear he was about to have death on his hands and I know there's nothing I can do to stop it.

My abductor laughs. "You think she's your little girl, but she's ours."

"Luke, look out!" I scream out.

A second man comes out of nowhere with a two by four in his hands, raised overhead as he swings it at Luke.

He ducks and delivers an uppercut to the man's stomach, dropping him with one punch.

"How many are there, Luna?"

"I don't know. I only saw the one," I muster.

As the second man coughs and reaches for his midsection, the first man tries to get to his feet, his eyes swollen shut from Luke's blows.

"It's time to end this right fucking now."

Luke swoops an arm around the fallen man's neck and quickly does the same to the first before he can get solid footing.

"Look away," he commands, and I do as I'm told.

I can hear Luke grunting as he squeezes tighter, not needing to look to know what's happening as he chokes both men out.

"Put them down, Luke!" another voice yells.

My head jerks to see a police officer with his gun trained on Luke.

"You kill them it's a double homicide."

"They took what's mine. I'm a judge, jury, and executioner. You want me to stop, you're going to have to kill me first."

My eyes dart back to Luke as he pulls the bodies in front of him, using them as a shield as I watch the last of the life go out of them. But Luke doesn't let go, he continues squeezing just in case.

"Holy shit. How many girls are down here?" the other cop

asks, the gun dropping to his side just before a whole slew of other officers come rushing to his side, mouthing a bevy of other profanities.

"Too many," one of the officers says.

"*One* is too many," Luke corrects. "It's our job to protect our women and we failed."

He releases his grip from around the two men, their lifeless bodies falling into a heap. Quickly he digs into one man's pocket, and then the other's, finding the keys and undoing my restraints.

He tosses the keys to another officer who quickly gets to work freeing the other women.

"You okay, baby?" he says, caressing my cheeks before his forehead finds mine. "I'm sorry I wasn't here sooner. I'm sorry this happened. I'm sorry—"

I bring my lips down on his, hard. "I'm thankful you found me. You saved me."

Then I pull my head back, run my fingers along my wrists, trying to wring out the pain before I cock back and slap him across the face.

"Why did you cheat on me…with a hooker!"

His eyebrow cocks and he looks at me quizzically.

"Cheat on you? What the hell are you talking about."

"That woman in the gas station bathroom. I *saw you*, Luke." I put my finger in his chest and he lowers his head, just shaking it in disbelief before he slowly raises it.

"What you must have seen was me not blowing the cover of

undercover Detective Aimee Johnson. The same woman who alerted me to this pile of garbage," he adds, motioning to the body lying in a pile on the ground with its accomplice.

I realize my mistake and there aren't words to say how sorry I am, but still...I try.

"I'm so sorry," I offer, and he accepts immediately, pulling me into a hug.

Long seconds pass before an officer yells, "Clear," apparently alerting us that there are no other predators here.

"How did you know to find me here?"

"I got video of the van you were..." his teeth grit as he has trouble continuing, but forces through the pain, "abducted in headed out this way. I used to come here as a kid, to try and get away from my father, from everything."

"My dad," I gasp, bringing my hands to my face.

"Don't worry about him. I'm getting you out of here and taking you to a hospital to get looked at."

"I'm okay. Just roughed up a little, but really I'm—"

"Your mine, and I take care of what's mine. Now don't try and protest. I'm getting you looked at...by a female doctor, to make sure."

He scoops me up in his arms and turns to leave, before stopping and kicking the man dressed in the Orphan Annie garb. Then he spits on his body. "Rot in hell, motherfucker, because that's where assholes like you who raise a hand to women, who harm them in any way, belong. Piece of shit."

He turns and carries me away from the most disgusting scene I've ever seen, but the most beautiful at the same time.

The other girls are being freed and looked after, and if there's any consolation, maybe it's that my kidnapping led to their rescue...to our rescue.

Because I've got my special protector looking out for me. My possessive policeman.

15

LUNA

I find myself back in the interrogation room, the space as cold and colorful as a sheet of notebook paper. The chair underneath me uneven, causing it to rock from side to side with each uneven breath I take.

"Just because Detective…" the police officer speaking with me pauses, "Luke, took you out of this room, doesn't mean, in any way, that you were free to go. You should have come back."

I look up at the public defender who simply raises his palms toward the sky as if to say he's got nothing to help me.

"I take responsibility for my actions, but as you know Luke can be very…convincing."

The door opens and a man motions for the interrogator to step in his direction. "One moment," he says, excusing himself and then proceeds to nod numerous times by the door while someone speaks quietly in his ear.

The officer returns and takes a seat at the table that's basically turned this boxlike enclosure into a pressure cooker, and I prepare to go over the specifics again, considering he seems to keep asking me the same questions thinking I'm going to give a different response or change my mind or something.

I've stayed steadfast in telling the truth, and wanting nothing more than to see Luke a request I've made numerous times but was quickly denied each and every time.

I want to make sure he's okay, and I need to apologize to him again. I can't believe I jumped to such a wild conclusion, even though it made sense based on what I thought I was seeing. None of this would have happened if I hadn't left the suite, which the police are saying was basically serving as a hideout and I was on the run after leaving the station hoisted over Luke's shoulder.

And then there was the worry about the way Luke took care of those two kidnappers in the abandoned mine. He should have just detained them, but he took the ultimate step and decided their fates for them.

"So, just once more for the record," he begins, and I exhale hard. "You'd never seen Mr. Darko before?"

"Who's Mr. Darko?"

"The person who was dressed up as the children's character commonly referred to as Little Orphan Annie."

"Never," I repeat for the umpteenth time.

"Nor were you familiar with Mr. Jankowitz?"

"That was his accomplice?"

"The man who had also taken up residence in the mine. Yes."

"Never."

The officer motions to my defender and they both step outside. Seconds later only the publicly appointed defender steps back in.

"You're free to go."

"What? Really?"

He nods. "Damn, you're a lucky one."

"I'm the lucky one," I hear Luke's unmistakable deep baritone just before he steps into the doorway in-between the attorney and myself, blocking him out entirely with his big body.

"Let's get outta here," he says, offering me his hand.

"Where to?" I readily accept.

"Anywhere but here."

"I hear that."

"You like ice cream?"

"Love it."

As we walk through the station I can't help but jump the gun. "What happened?"

"I'll fill you in in a second," he says as we walk out the front door.

"And you'll fill me in right now." We both freeze as we're confronted by my dad, arms across his chest as he taps his toe on the ground. His eyebrows raise and he cocks his head.

"Let's all sit down over here," Luke offers, motioning toward the park bench just in front of the station.

"No, Luke. You're going to tell me what the hell's going on," my dad says, not budging. "And you're going to tell me now."

16

LUKE

I just stood there, refusing to even rub the spot on my jaw where Steven had just decked me. Strangely, it didn't hurt. If anything it felt good, because it told me that maybe my best friend did actually care about his daughter after all. It seemed he'd been neglecting her all these years, so it was good to finally see some sort of outward expression of him caring about her well-being, even if it did come at my expense.

Looking to the side I see Luna squatting and raising nervously the way a child might if she needed to go to the bathroom. But I know what she's really expressing, the anxiety of how this is all going to turn out. "Everything's going to be okay," I comfort her, which only draws me another punch from her dad. Apparently, my words make him feel like his first punch didn't hit home hard enough.

"All right, Steven. That's enough. I let you get your aggression out. You hit me again and I'm going to hit back...a lot harder." The truth was I wouldn't hit him. There would be no need. I could lock him up in a hold that didn't injure either of us but would restrain him. But my words should be enough.

And judging from the look on his face they are. He takes a step back, his mouth opening like he wants to ask a question but he's not sure where to begin.

I don't talk first or prepare some sort of rebuttal. Truth is the best response, and I'm ready to tell him whatever he wants to know and to be honest about it too. I'm not about to deny what I feel for Luna, and I want him to see that she belongs to me now, no matter what anyone else in the world thinks they can do about it.

Luna steps forward taking a spot by my side. I intertwine my fingers in hers, pulling her little body in closer, but not too close. I don't want to piss off Steven any more than he already is. He is my best friend and my future father in law, even though just thinking of that title for him seems completely outrageous. But I'm not going to disrespect him. Looking at his face I can see the wheels of his brain turning, knowing he's trying to figure this all out, trying to understand what's happening. I don't need to shove my affection for his daughter smack dab in his face. That's only going to upset, frustrate, and anger him more.

I need him to calm down and think logically, not get more riled up.

"How long has this been going on?" he asks flatly, his voice not tipping off his thoughts one bit.

"It hasn't been going on at all," I start. "It just happened. My protective instincts took over and—"

"So this is a short-term thing?"

"No, dad," Luna pipes up, her body moving forward slightly. "I've been in love with Luke since I knew what love was. I know that probably sounds strange to you, but you have to know I never said anything about it, never acted on it, and Luke definitely never displayed any kind of romantic feelings toward me until my birthday party."

"Her *eighteenth* birthday party. As if you were just waiting for her to be legal so you could do what you already had planned." Steven shakes his head.

"It's not like that at all. I won't lie...there was something about that day, something about the way she dressed and acted. Not only had she become an adult in number, but in the ways, she lived, acted, talked. She was always wise beyond her age, Steven. We both know that. If she wasn't you wouldn't have felt comfortable leaving her home alone."

"Don't you dare turn this on me."

"I'm not. Don't get defensive." I pause, realizing I'm not helping to keep the situation toned down. "All I'm saying is, the trust you displayed in her, treating her like an adult all those years led her to mature quickly, much more so than her peers."

"To the point, she wants to date a man twice her age?"

"Not date," I quickly correct. "L... It's more than that. I can't speak for Luna. It's not right. She's an adult and can say whatever she wants to say. But I can speak for myself and I'll say unequivocally that this is real, lasting and I love her with everything I've got. Everything I have. And as you know I've never been with a woman. You're always teasing me about it and telling me it must be because there's a perfect one out there for me somewhere. Well...you were right."

Steven looks off into the distance and Luna's hand grips mine harder, specifically when I used the word love. He takes a few steps toward the side, then circles the area, just looking

114

off in the distance as he processes everything that's happening.

"You know this isn't something I can just flat out accept. You know that, right?"

"I don't know that, but I understand. I also ask that you have some understanding for us and at least approach this with an open mind. I would say give us some time to prove to you that this is everything I say it is, but I don't feel like I have time. I feel like I've wasted forty-one years of it already and I need to make up for that time I lost."

"Forty-one, Luna," Steven repeats my age aloud, wincing. "Are you sure?"

"Absolutely," she says immediately.

"You know, Steven. I don't mean to tell you how to be a father. I've never tried. But do you realize your daughter was abducted and held by two at large serial killers and your first concern is who she can and can't be with? I'm not Sigmund Freud, and I'm not trying to sound like a jerk, but it's the things in our childhood that often shape us. Part of what Luna needs might just be someone who actually cares about her for her, her well-being, her safety. Someone who's always got her back, a protector, and dare I say a paternal figure."

"I'm right here," she says, tugging at my arm. "Wow, that was kind of embarrassing."

Finally, Steven nods. "You're right. I wasn't the best of father's and that's something Luna might be searching for."

"Hello!" She jumps in. "Please don't talk about me like you're both my dad and as if I wasn't standing right here."

I'm not sure why but all three of us bust out laughing for a quick second before things go back to being serious, although not as tense as they were before.

"I agree. I·won't stand for this, but I will kneel. Because I don't know what Luna's searching for, but I know what I've found…the most amazing woman in the world."

My words are a little bit cryptic, but I reveal their true meaning as I take a knee and pop open the top of the black, velvet box I bought last week the day after her birthday. I've been carrying it with me ever since, and most importantly isn't the box, but what's inside.

The sun catches the princess cut diamond ring and Luna's hands shoot to her mouth, covering it in shock.

"Just like the cut of this diamond, *you* are a princess…my princess. And just as this diamond will last forever, so will my love for you. I want you to wear this for eternity, so whenever any sees it they will know you are loved, respected, and most importantly that you belong to me. Mine," I can't help but growl. "You've already made me the happiest man to ever walk the face of the earth. Now make me your forever. Because that's exactly how long you'll always be mine. You're my everything so be my wife, my love, the mother of my children…forever. Will you marry me, princess?"

Luna

I nod, slowly at first and then feverishly. Luke reaches for me and I offer him my shaking hand. He slides the ring on and I know it will never come off. Perfect, because it's a perfect fit.

Picking me up he spins me around like a little girl and then as my feet swing out he slows, centrifugal force taking over, he wraps me up in a big body hug, my feet not touching the ground. Even if they were I'd never know it. I'm on cloud nine, thanks to him.

He stamps his lips across mine and my eyes close as I already begin to dream of the next chapter in this fairytale romance, and it's all thanks to my possessive policeman.

"I love you," he says.

"I love you."

EPILOGUE

LUNA

One month later

I sip my coffee at an empty table across from the police station. Why I'm drinking coffee I don't know. I'm already totally wired after the news I just got and if anything I should be downing an alcoholic beverage to calm myself before I tell Luke.

But I'm too young for alcohol, it sounds icky to me too, and I know Luke would bend me over his knee if he caught me breaking any of his rules, or the law...especially now that he's been reinstated with full pay as a cop, not that we need the money.

Apparently, those two serial killers each had one million dollar rewards on their heads for their arrest or capture. Luke didn't exactly arrest them or capture them, but he did get them off the street, and the F.B.I. paid up. After taxes, we walked with a million, which seems to be more than enough to start saving for our first child's education fund, the same child that Luke swears is already inside my belly despite the fact that he has no actual proof...at least he didn't until I break the news the doctor gave me an hour ago.

Fortunately, my dad's come to terms with Luke and me as well. It didn't happen overnight, but after a couple of weeks of 'processing' everything, he realized it makes complete sense, no matter how awkward it might first appear.

I stab my spoon into the sprinkles on top of my coffee and do some processing of my own, having just completed my first day at the newsroom where Luke got me an entry-level position. He promised me he could get me started off higher, but I insisted on the bottom. I want to prove myself and work my way up. If I get a handout or what's perceived as an unfair advantage from the start that reputation will never leave me. I want everyone to know I earn what I get.

The funny thing is even starting at the bottom I can see I'm not going to be treated like the lowest member on the totem pole. Everyone was so nice and accommodating today, to a fault even. I just smirk, knowing that Luke surely had something to do with that.

"Hey there," a voice says behind me. "Anybody sitting here?"

I don't recognize the voice and turn to see a boy about my age trying to look all cocky. I recognize him as the star of the football team. He's big, strong, and definitely the target of a lot of girls back at school. The only thing is I'm no longer in high school, having graduated, even a bit ahead of schedule, and I have the kind of strong man that's rough and ready, not a polished Abercrombie and Fitch version.

"No, but I prefer to be alone. Thank you," I say flatly, yet respectfully.

"If no one's sitting there, then I guess you were saving it for me."

He slides into the booth and I wonder how he's not getting the picture.

"I was just going," I say, reaching for my things when suddenly his hand comes out and he grabs my wrist. It's only then I realize I had tucked my hands into my sweater and he can't see my engagement ring. I didn't do it intentionally, of course, it's just that sometimes it's chilly and I like to snuggle up with whatever I have handy. No blanket? I guess a sweater has to do, which is exactly what happened in this particular case.

My eyes look left and right and I don't see anyone in the shop. The single employee must be in the backroom doing something, so screaming isn't going to solve anything. Then again screaming isn't really my style. The guy is certainly being aggressive, but I'm not worried. There's this strength that resides within me, maybe even a false sense of security at times that makes me think I'm tougher than I am, just knowing that Luke's my man. But he's not here right now, and I need to remember that.

Or is he?

The bell on the door rings and his big body steps into the shop, which is strange considering there's no way I'd ever guess he'd be caught dead in a place decorated in pink and pastels that serves coffees on little animal shaped saucers.

"My boyfriend is here and he won't appreciate what you're doing," I warn.

"You've been sitting here alone since I came in. You don't have a boyfriend, and I don't want to be your boyfriend either. I'm just interested in…having a little fun. Whaddya say?"

The sound of Luke's boots gobbling up tiles comes to a stop as he stops right behind the city's star quarterback, casting a shadow over him and the entire table.

"I want to have some fun. Let's play," he says, grabbing the boy's arm and twisting it behind his back in one move, his grip easily releasing me as Luke turkey wings his arm and jams his bent wrist into his back.

"You never put your hands on a woman unless she specifically invites you to. See this is what it feels like when someone twice your size touches you without your permission. Understand…*son?*"

"That's my throwing arm!" he protests, that deep voice he tried to throw my way when he wanted to sit down completely gone, a high-pitched whine replacing it.

"Oh, you like to throw. What a coincidence. Me too. Let's see how far I can throw."

"Put me down, old man."

"If you insist."

Luke drags him toward the door and uses his head to push it open before rocking back on his heels and chucking him into the street.

The boy rushes to stand but he's clearly off balance, tripping and falling before trying again and then scurrying off to who knows where.

"Was that really necessary?" I tease, knowing that nothing I say or do will ever stop Luke from protecting what's his.

"Absolutely. He didn't see your ring?"

"I had my hand tucked in my sweatshirt. I was cold." I roll my bottom lip in Luke's direction.

"Well, Daddy's here now and he's got a big bear hug with his little girl's name on it."

He pulls me in close and the warmth coming from his body is like that of a warm stove on a winter's night. I bury my head in his chest and melt into his body.

"How was your first day at work?" he asks.

"Great, and I even had a quick minute to swing by the doctor's office on the way over here."

"You're not feeling well?" He puts his hand on my forehead and concern spreads across his face.

"No, I feel great." I pause, realizing I need an answer to a question before I break the news about the pregnancy. "How did you know I was here? How did you know to come, and so fast to boot?"

"It's my job to make sure you're safe, and I take my job *very* seriously."

"I'm being serious, Luke." I playfully swat him on the arm, but his look is stone cold.

"So am I."

I let it go, knowing I may never know and I don't need to. All I need to know is the man has a sixth sense when it comes to keeping me safe, and probably a lot of technology and eyes on the street making sure I'm safe too. All that matters is he cares about me and puts me first, in all ways.

Now it's time to tell him about our first, in a totally different way.

"You know how you're always saying you're sure I got pregnant the first time we were together?"

"You did."

"Okay, Mr. Smarty Pants. Well...you were right."

He just nods. "Damn right." He pauses. "I didn't need any confirmation to know what I already knew. But now that we have the word from the doctor we need to celebrate."

"Aren't you excited?" I ask, surprised he seems so even keel.

"Excited? More than you could know. Outwardly showing it? Not just yet."

"What is that supposed to mean?"

"You mean everything to me, and having a family with you is the ultimate. This is the pinnacle of my life, as it would be with any man's. But there can only be one man to have you, and I'm still slightly in shock that somehow that man is me. It's hard to process and with great power comes great responsibility."

"Power? As in power over me?"

"Just the opposite. Daddy draws all his power from you, and then energy his little girl fills his with each and every day. If only you knew what you really mean to me, to this world, to your father, to us all."

"You tell me every hour of the day."

"Clearly not enough, because it's not fully sinking in. All I'm trying to say is... don't worry about it. There aren't words.

All that matters is I love you, I love us," he corrects, putting his hand on my belly, "And that you're mine."

"Yours," I agree.

"And that's why I'm at a loss for words."

"Well just kiss me then."

"With pleasure, but first, let me be the first to call you by another name."

"Which little girl name did you think up now?" I tease.

"Not a little girl name, but the name our little girls and boys will call you, but I want the honors first…mom."

"Thank you, Daddy."

I wrap my arms around him and he kisses me like the world is on fire. And the crazy part is that if it was, I know he'd do whatever it takes to keep me safe, because his blood boils hot for me…my possessive policeman.

EXTENDED EPILOGUE

LUKE

Five years later

I pull the squad car up and over the curb, so excited to make this bust that I damn near ram the grill into the brick wall of the building a foot in front of it.

Stepping out of the Crown Victoria, my first finger and thumb adjust my Ray-Bans down and I look over the top of the gold frames at the young woman selling herself out here today.

I push my glasses back into position and take my nightstick from the holster on my belt, tapping it into the palm of my other hand as I approach in full uniform.

"I'm going to need to see some identification...miss," I order flatly.

"I'm sorry officer," Luna says, wrapping a lock of her strawberry red hair around her index finger while she blows a bubble with her Bubbalicious gum. "I'm afraid I don't have any...other than these."

Her fingers curl around the plunging neckline of her sequined top, showing the ample cleavage she currently has thanks to the recent birth of our second son, and third child overall, Liam. "Maybe we can settle this problem," her eyes drifting to my groin, "without going downtown?"

"Whoa there, miss," I continue role-playing. "Are you trying to bribe an officer of the law?"

"That depends, officer. Are you interested or not?"

"Against the wall and spread 'em," I command. She keeps her eyes focused on me as her body rotates one hundred and eighty degrees.

"What, are you gonna...frisk me?"

I slap on the cuffs and press the nightstick into her back. My other hand reaches around and I frame her jaw with my hand, applying a small amount of pressure as I tilt her face up to mine. "I'm going to do a whole lot more than that... little girl."

Her breath hitches and her cuffed hands come together, fisting my cock over the top of my uniform. "Are you gonna use your weapon on me? The one that's already locked and loaded?" she continues, her hands moving down and feeling that my balls are already pulled uptight at this fantasy we're acting out. "Isn't it dangerous to have a loaded weapon so close to a suspect?"

"It is. And that's why you're going to unload it for me."

The nightstick in her back nudges her downward and I carefully guide her to her knees, rotating her body ninety degrees so she's parallel to the building now.

Her baby blues drop down to my zipper, her tongue sliding

out between her bee stung lips, licking the top and then the bottom, lubricating the entrance I'm so damn ready to claim.

I lift a hand, pinching my zipper between two calloused fingers, and lower it...slowly.

Ramming my hand down my pants, I fist my rod, pulling it up and over the top of my boxer briefs waistband and pressing it down so it's horizontal. I'm so fucking hard my member wants to go vertical, but I manage to line it up with her freshly moistened lips and she surges forward, taking my cock in her gaping little mouth.

I sink in a few more pulsating inches, my naughty little girl sucking me off so fast I'm damn near ready to snap already.

"Better than a citation, isn't it little girl?"

"Uh huh," she mumbles.

"Good. Keep sucking it sloppy because you want all the lubrication you can get when this dirty cop gives you the prison experience as part of your punishment."

The filthy promise falling from my mouth elicits a moan from her as she bobs on my fat girth, willing as much of it as she can in between her lips, her cheeks hollowing out as she makes it happen.

The sight of her struggling to take in all of me in her mouth is easily enough to make me come, but instead, I bite down on my tongue, the metallic taste of blood a feeble attempt to take my mind off what my body is demanding...but thankfully it works.

My free hand comes to rest on top of her head, those eyes that could take me to my knees staring up at me, her pupils dilating.

Rolling my hips toward her mouth, she takes in even more of me, whimpering as her tongue bathes my flesh, lips suctioning and thankfully her teeth staying back and away. No clipping my foreskin. My little girl knows how to please her daddy.

Knowing I'm damn close I slide my cock from her mouth and her face instantly pouts, all her features scrunching up in the middle as she makes a protesting sound.

I lean down and kiss her swollen lips, then fist her throat, applying pressure upward on her jaw as I lift her back to her feet.

"You like it rough, officer. Don't you?"

"Not as much as you do you dirty little girl? Word on the street is this is the best pussy on the planet, but that no one's ever entered that back door."

"Word on the street is often wrong...but in this case it's right."

I gently squeeze the front of her into the wall, her body shaking with excitement as I use my nightstick to lift up her too short skirt.

"What do we have here?"

"An illegal search and seizure," she foreshadows, and I can't help but smirk.

"Oh, I already found what I'm looking for." I tap the tip of my nightstick on her puckered hole. "And when I stick my rod inside it for the first time, I can guarantee your body is going to seize up, my tight little streetwalker."

Sliding a knee in between her legs I push open her legs

wider, then tap the insides of her transparent heels with the outside of my boots. And her legs go wider yet.

Bringing one hand down on her pantyless cheeks, I knead a perfect globe before pulling the flesh away from her body, separating her glutes roughly and giving myself a look at her untouched entrance.

"Here," I offer, bringing the nightstick around in front of her face. "Bit down on this."

Immediately her neck stretches for it, as she takes it in her mouth like a dog seizes a bone.

I bend down, spitting on her puckered hole before rising back up. I need to make sure she's properly lubricated. I'm harder than a rock and that asshole is untouched.

Do we like a little pain with our pleasure? Absolutely. Would I ever actually hurt her. Hell fucking no.

I line up my crown with her opening. "Take a deep breath in and hold it. You'll know when to let it out."

She does as she's told and I slowly inch my hips forward, wedging my cock between her cheeks and entering the forbidden land I'm about to claim as mine.

"Fuck. So. Damn. Tight," I moan, barely even three inches deep.

I remind myself that her pleasure always comes first. As she exhales into the nightstick and the sound of her teeth trying to tear into the metal dissipates, I slide it from in from her once-locked jaw, turning it vertically and begin sawing it through her folds, as my hips rock back and forth as I fill her bottom with my dick.

Her knees bend as her hips push forward.

"Ride it for, Daddy," I demand into her ear. "Fuck it while I defile you."

Her breath hitches and from the side of her I notice a tear slide from the corner of her eye. "So fucking good, Daddy."

"This is what would have happened if I would have taken you downtown, put you in a cell in the general population, you naughty girl, you."

She has no idea how hard it is for me to hold my climax right now. A grumble continuously rolls out from my chest as I continue working my inches inside her.

My body folds in half and I spit on her entrance, inching inside even deeper with a low, guttural sound of a man possessed by the devil. A man who's on the cusp of turning into an absolute beast. A man who needs to be locked up for the filthy thoughts slamming inside his head right now.

"Daddy's going to play a game now...see how deep we can get. Are you ready little girl?"

"Uh huh," she whimpers, and I bite down on her exposed shoulder, my teeth sinking into the tip of the hibiscus petal tattoo she's added to her body. Three blossoms, one for each of our trifecta of children.

The mounds of her sweet ass press into my hips as I run my hand down the perfect curve of her lower back. The side of her face is pressed to the brick, ragged breaths escaping her as her muscles clench so fucking tight around my dick I can hardly breathe.

I turn the angle of the nightstick, hitting her clit just right. "There. Right there," she moans. "Oh, Daddy. I'm...I'm...I'm coming!"

Her body seizes as she shudders, her cream coming out in spurts and immediately I explode inside her tiny asshole, overflowing her back end while I shout curses into the air as a white river trickles down her leg.

My hand slides around the front of her body, cupping her breasts over her top before I reach her neck, cupping her throat.

I turn her head so her ear is directly in line with my mouth. "Mine," I remind her, before giving her earlobe a tug with the tips of my teeth. "Forever."

"Yours," she confirms, and it's what I need to hear...always. It comforts me, eases me, and reminds me that I'm doing my job as a husband, father, and Daddy. As her protector, provider, biggest fan and encourager, and partner in this crazy journey called life.

"Consider your debt to society paid, you naughty little girl."

"Yes, officer." She smirks and quickly I stamp her lips with a frantic kiss, our tongues exploring deeply.

Our heads pull away with the sound of the vacuum seal of our faces being snapped and I slide out of her.

We quickly straighten our clothes.

"That was one hell of a fantasy," she says. "Seemed real to me."

I pause, fisting her hair and pulling her in close. "Everything about the way I feel for you, about our family is real...every moment of every day which still seems like a fantasy so damn much I need to pinch myself."

She reaches around and does the honor, before darting off. "Catch me if you can, officer."

Oh, I'll catch her all right, because she's mine…and she's never getting away. I locked her up and threw away the key a long time ago. My love is a maximum security prison with no escape, not that she'd ever want to because I dedicate every waking moment to making her happy, because it completes and fulfills me. That's what Daddy's do.

Forever and always.

EXTENDED EPILOGUE

LUNA

Ten years later

I adjust the fancy Herman Miller Aeron chair underneath me while a makeup artist touches me up and another straightens my outfit.

"In three...two..." the producer counts down.

I look to the side of the camera and see my entire family there, cheering me on. They've all got smiles on their faces. Little Layla and Lily have their cell phones out. Lucy is bent at the knees, hands clapped as she watches with excitement. Our twins Lydia and Leo hold hands with their mouths slightly open. Levi just stands there beaming, while Luke holds baby Logan in his arms, and Lucas and Liam each have a hand wrapped around the other's shoulders.

All eyes on mama.

It's taken a decade but it's been more than worth it. No matter how long this journey to become a news anchor woman has become, it could never top my family.

As proud as I am for working my way up, being a top crime reporter for five years, and everything I've achieved at work…it's nothing without my support system, our team of 'L's' here to share it all with.

Luke has been amazing. He's scaled back his detective work to make it fair that I quit reporting on crimes. He said there's no point in chasing around weirdos out in the street when I already have him, and his crazed ways, to deal with at home. Even after ten years the man still can't get enough of me, telling me I need to *gain* more weight so I don't get hurt when he loses his mind on a daily basis, taking me from more angles, in more positions, and in more rooms in our house than should be mathematically possible.

He chauffeurs the kids to practices, takes care of a lot of the things at home, and rubs my feet, and encourages me after a long day. He's always there to tell me I can quit whenever I want, that he's the man and he can, and does, provide. We've never even spent a penny of my earnings, just socking it away in the bank so the kids can have money for their educations and first homes when the times come. And oh how quickly does the time fly by.

The big sign that reads 'live' flashes and I introduce the lead story before handing it over to my co-anchor. My eyes catch one of our producers looking down at his phone, but no longer than a second because Luke slaps him in the back of his head and then points to his eyes and then to me, telling the man where to focus his attention.

That's my Luke all right. He's taught all our boys about respecting women, in all ways, and he makes sure all men, whether family or not, respect me and the girls. It's in his blood, his D.N.A., and everything he does. And it's just another thing I love about him.

My eyes drift over to my dad, who's leaning against the wall. He just lifts a single hand and waves at me. My hand goes to raise, but then I forget I'm on live TV. I flash him a smile instead and he gives me a wink.

He's also scaled back his work a lot. Turns out he likes being a grandparent more than he ever did being a parent. Then again, he's been a much better dad than he ever has been… ever since his best friend claimed me a decade ago.

My attention turns back to Luke, whose eyes rake over my body, stopping just under the desk. I feel my cheeks heat, remembering what he told me before we all piled into the van and drove over.

"You better not have any panties on because I'm going to be the first to congratulate you after your first show as an anchor. And by anchor I mean anchor my tongue to your channel, suck up all your juices, and wipe your climax clean with my face."

He can be so vulgar, and so darn exciting, all in the same breath…and he's been doing it for what seems like forever now.

I wiggle in my seat, pretending to do my best Sharon Stone impression from Basic Instinct. Luke steps in front of the male producer who he just told to watch me, and now he's blocking his line of sight.

My producer throws up his hands in frustration, but he knows better than to mess with Luke. And hopefully Luke knows there's no way anyone can actually see under the table. It's specifically designed for wardrobe malfunctions.

But you can't tell him that. He is, and always will be my possessive policeman.

And as soon as the show raps thirty minutes later he comes rushing up onto the set, scooping me up and delivering an arresting kiss smack dab on my lips.

"Daddy's hungry, little girl."

"Luke!" I protest, fumbling with my microphone, trying to get it off knowing it's still a hot mic, broadcasting sound.

But nobody bats an eye. They know better than to stick their nose into the family den that's protected by our proud papa bear. Not only that, I think people already know we have a special dynamic, the one that completes us in all ways.

It used to make us seem strange to other people, but after all these years I catch them looking at us with envy.

That's how it works when you're different. High risk, high reward. And this policeman is the ultimate thief who got away...with my heart.

And he's got every intention of possessing, protecting, and cherishing it...forever.

"Way to go, mom!"

"Great job, mom!"

"You look, so beautiful mommy!"

"Congratulations, baby girl. Daddy is so proud of you," he whispers through the chaos and congratulations, his deep voice cutting through all the rest.

"Thank you, Daddy."

"Good girl...now it's time for Daddy to give you your reward," he promises, carrying me back to my dressing room to congratulate me in another way.

As he throws me over his shoulder like a caveman I see my father step in and round up the kids, moving them over to the congratulatory cake Luke must have had prepared for me.

He's truly thought of everything, but all that really matters is how much he's always thinking about us...his family, his everything.

I love this man...my possessive policeman.

"I love you," he growls as he kicks open my dressing room door.

"And I love you."

THE END

~~~

Thanks for reading! Get free books from time to time by signing up for my mailing list. You'll also be alerted when my next story goes live. Sign up on the link below...

www.subscribepage.com/lenalittle

Printed in Great Britain
by Amazon